# BLOOD
## *on the*
# BLADE

A NOVEL
*By Lloyd Hollis Crooks*

WAYNE BRATHWAITE PUBLISHERS

519 EAST 26TH STREET
BROOKLYN, NEW YORK 11210
E-mail: crooksgg519@aol.com
Phone: 1-718-693-6710
www.lloydholliscrooks.com

BLOOD ON THE BLADE
A Novel by
LLOYD HOLLIS CROOKS


PATRICIA BELCON, Ph.D
*Editor*

Library of Congress Control No. 2016911541
ISBN 978-0966629613
Printed in the United States
Designed by: Nkko Designs

THE MOTHERS OF GOWER'S WELL ROAD, FYZABAD, TRINIDAD, WEST INDIES: Leoni Crooks Sears; Lyris George; Albertha Umy James; Elaine Trotman; Delcina Campbell; June Fordrass; Etta Tuitt; Miss Jules; Rosalind Scott; Doris Pierre; Mother Gerald; Lottie Dublin; Miss. Duntin; Miss Roberts; Miss Alexander; Miss Lett; Miss Smith; Miss Sammy; Miss Williams; Miss Fraser; Miss Ramkesoon; Miss Sooji; Rose Brathwaite; Miss Boolitan; Miss Chinee; Miss Thomas; Miss Caro; Rosa Best; Miss Dora; Miss Briggs; Miss Joseph; Miss Cannigator; Miss Maharaj; Miss Boodoosingh; Miss Ritika; Miss Briggs; Miss Emmanuel; Miss Pascall; Miss Mary; Lina McQulkin; Miss Isaac; Miss Marcell; Miss Mark; Miss Reese; Miss Francis; Miss Lambert; and all the Mothers who are dead and those whose names I've forgotten, who had disciplined me for my own good; and who had been kind to me when I was a little barefooted boy in short pants and bracers.

## Acknowledgments

Thank you, Dr. Patricia Belcon, for your editing skills applied to my book. You served as an amazing muse when we chatted as buddies about our varied childhoods and our parenting. Thank you, Leonora Boyce-Crooks, Industrial Relations Activist, for sharing with me your hiking experiences of your travels through all the routes to Maracas Bay. Being away from Trinidad and Tobago for fifty years, your knowledge saved me from tedious research to find those places for inclusion in my book.

Thank you, Austin "Elder T" Tuitt, for allowing me to use a poem from *Pearls of Inspiration*.

Thank you, Edward Noble, Reynold James, Anthony George, Steve Crooks, Ulric "Boong" Dublin, Austin "Skylark" Tuitt, Fritz Fraser, Jonathan "Boozie" Valley, Alvin Thomas, Lloyd Mason and Kenwyn Joseph for reminding me of the crazy incidents that only we, boys of Gower's Well Road, Fyzabad, know that I had completely forgotten. Your friendship over sixty years has been invaluable.

And, finally, I also want to give a special thanks to the book designer, Nandi Keyi, a true professional.

*Friends only I strive to create*
*While in service I am entwined*
*Always leaving my door to reconciliation*
*ajar,*
*Beckoning my adversary to enter.*

Austin H. Tuitt

# 1

The Canadian Missionary woman, known as Miss Kumari by the Sunday school children, stood with a permanent smile in a print frock falling below her knees on the jagged concrete steps of the Canadian Mission Presbyterian Church on Lamtack Hill, Fyzabad, a little oil town in South Trinidad, West Indies. In Fyzabad in the 1930's, race relations was not always parlayed as cultural diffusion that was worthy of spreading goodwill among its mixed population of the dominant two races—the East Indians (Indians) and Creoles (Blacks); sometimes race relations was like a bitter pill that the two races were forced to swallow, knowing fully well when they swallow that pill they will be infected with hate.

Padma Kumari waited patiently to greet every Indian child who came to Sunday school to learn Hindi; and she was shocked beyond words when Alex, the only Creole boy, came for the first time to Sunday school to learn Hindi. Alex's Mother, known as Madam Joe by the villagers, sent Alex to learn Hindi because she was aware of some of her Indian neighbors' vindictive threats against her, especially a man named Zoffi Thakur. Knowing Alex's precociousness and acute sensibility, Madam Joe knew he would learn Hindi quickly; he would interpret what the Indian neighbors say in Hindi about her; and he would tell her in English.

Eight-year-old Alex always stood out at the end of the line every Sunday when he greeted Miss Kumari, and he looked at her admiringly. There came a time in Fyzabad when Black people were called Negroes and Colored people. But Alex remembered only the time when Black people as he were called

Creole people in the 1930s when he was born; and later in life Alex was told by atheist John Jules, his go-to for general knowledge, that "Creole originated from two words: Spanish *criar*, to create, and *colono*, a colonist, into the word *criollo*."

Alex did not care to know the meaning of those foreign words which he could not pronounce. But he believed Jules's indigenous interpretation of the word *Creole*: "Alex, those English-expatriate bastards from England working in the oilfields with your Father and me would not call us Niggers in front our face because they want us to climb those high derricks that they are afraid to climb, so they call us by the fancy name *Creole* as a bribe for us to climb those high, slippery derricks."

Alex loved the way Miss Kumari greeted him every Sunday-school morning: "Alex, you are such a nice Creole boy;" and she always put a dinner mint in his hand. Most times the wrappers were warm as if she had those mints in her hand two hours ago especially for him. He didn't know whether she gave him the dinner mints for perfect attendance or for the way he completed all his Hindi home lessons ahead of time. He told Madam Joe, "Mother, Miss Kumari likes the way my feet shine with coconut oil, and she tells me I'm a good-mannered Creole boy because I always wipe the mud off my feet on the door mat before I go in the church to sit. And, Mother, she said even though I am a little Creole boy I sing *Jesus Loves Me This I Know* in Hindi better than the Indian children. She tells us, children, she likes Fyzabad better than the place she came from in Naparima; and she hopes the Canadian Missionary Board will never transfer her from Fyzabad to any place else."

Fyzabad, nicknamed Fyzo, is named after Faizabad, a village in India. It is the most historical town in the twin island of Trinidad and Tobago; and it is the birth place of the trade union movement in Trinidad and Tobago founded by Tubal Uriah Butler. When Fyzabadians hail for a taxi to take them home from San Fernando, the industrial capital, where they go to shop for fridges, jewelry from Y. D. Lima, and other expensive items, they hail for a taxi singing, "Yo-go-in-to-Fyzo."

Calypsonian Skylark, a naturalized native of Fyzabad, and the best known calypsonian in South Trinidad, taught Alex how to vamp a calypso background in an upbeat tempo with his harmonica; and when Alex became proficient in Hindi, he sang all Skylark's calypsos in Hindi. One day Alex asked, "Mr. Skylark, why did your Mother give you that funny name?"

"Alex, my Mother gave that nice name because a skylark is a beautiful bird that flies high up in the sky; it has the sweetest singing voice of all birds; and I sing as sweetly as a skylark. That's why my Mother gave me that nice name."

"I like your name now, Mr. Skylark."

In Sunday school Padma Kumari told her class Fyzabad was founded by Reverend Kenneth J. Grant, a Presbyterian missionary; and the purpose of the Fyzabad settlement was to separate the Christian Indians from the unconverted Hindu and Muslim population; and she emphasized she was sent to Fyzabad to make sure the "converted Hindu and Muslim children" remain in the Presbyterian's faith after she taught them about Christianity. Nonetheless, she knew some of her students will return to their original faiths.

That knowledge perked Alex's interest. "Miss Kumari, did Reverend Grant tell you to separate us, Creole children, from all the Indian children?" Alex stood erect, his coarse, sun-burned hair combed with a center part that showed his clean skull, waited on an answer from Miss Kumari. Her long hair was secured in an almost invisible hair net. Most of the girls' hair was long with the scent of coconut oil mixed with washed lard. Some of the boys' hair was cut like Tarzan's, others were crew cut.

Miss Kumari smiled before she replied. "Alex Sears, that's a good question. Reverend Grant is dead. But when the Canadian Mission Board Director sent me to Fyzabad, they never told me anything about the history of the Creole people. But I know the history of a great Creole man named Tubal Uriah Butler. Butler told the white people from England who own the oilfields that they have to pay all the oilfield workers—Indian and Creole—

more money, and give them better working conditions. And you, Alex, an intelligent Creole boy, will one day become as great as Mr. Butler, a great Creole hero."

"And why do the Indian people call Creole Butler a nigger, and he did so much good for them?"

"Creole people call Indian people like me coolies."

"My Mother calls neighbor Thakur a coolie when she is annoyed with him."

"If I'm annoyed with your Mother for not sending you on time for Sunday school, would your Mother call me a coolie?"

"I will ask her when I go home."

"Alex, a coolie is a person who totes load on his head. Do I carry load on my head when I am teaching you?"

"No, Miss Kumari. But why we call all you people with long hair coolies, and you call us with curly, curly hair niggers?"

"Next Sunday when we sing, in Hindi, *Jesus Loves all the Little Children in the World*, I will let all the Indian children know that all the Creole children in the world are all one people in the eyes of God. None is better than the other, and Mr. Butler is a great Creole hero for all the people of Fyzabad."

"My Father told me a lot about Mr. Butler. On June 19, Butler Day, my Father takes me by Charlie King Corner; and he tells me why the people of Fyzabad burned Charlie King to ashes during the Butler oilfield strike. Whenever I asked my Father if he was one of the strikers who burned Corporal Charlie King to ashes because Charlie King wanted to jail the strikers, my Father shakes his head like this for me to see."

Miss Kumari shook her head two ways: "Alex, your Father shook his head this way, or like this way?" She turned her head from left to right, and from right to left to indicate if his Father said yes or no.

"I can't remember now, Miss Kumari."

The children's laughter was boisterous. Miss Kumari ended Sunday school with praises to Alex. She was shocked by the historical knowledge he knew of Fyzabad and the way he expressed himself at age eight. She put two dinner mints into his both palms; and as Alex rushed down Lamtack Hill to go home and give his big brother, Paul, a dinner mint, an Indian boy shouted, "Nigger, don't come back to our church. I will beat you up."

"Toby, don't say that! When Alex comes to Sunday school next week, I want you to apologize to him," Miss Kumari said.

Alex told his Mother what Toby said. He refused to go back to Sunday school, but he practiced his Hindi with neighbor Mike who taught him to curse in Hindi. His Mother enrolled him at the Canadian Mission Primary School, and he had many Indian friends. One day he was shocked to hear drunken neighbor Cyril singing, with a calypso beat, "Jesus hates all the coolie children in the world." He told Cyril, "You are a bad man. I will tell my Mother not to give you any food when you come to beg; and if she gives you food, I'll spit in it."

Six years had passed, and Alex fell in love with Kristen, an Indian girl, who attended Sunday school with him. He dreamed of her every night. In his room the hot zinc roof heated his body, and his mind connived for clean thoughts. Then he heard his Mother's voice as he rested his head on the pillow. "What the hell Zoffi Thakur is sharpening day in and day out?"

The grinding noise never ceased. Alex went to bed hearing that grinding noise. He awoke hearing that noise louder. He spoke to himself. "Is Ziffo Thakur sharpening his machete again to kill somebody?" Fyzabadians keep their grudge for years, and Alex was wondering who is on Thakur's grudge list.

In Fyzabad, the machete had many names: cutlass, gillpin, poonyah, and the "coolie gun," a name coined by Steve Crooks who lived in the eternal-mud track, Anthony George who lived on the edge of the alligator dam, and Reynold James who lived on a mound in the graveled road. They called themselves the Terrible Trio. People who lived in mud tracks came at nights and scraped the gravel off the graveled road to put on their mud tracks. When Reynold was a little boy, he called out, "Thiefs, stop thiefing me mudder gravel;" and the thieves replied, "This is County Council's gravel, not your mother's gravel. Time to sleep, little boy."

The Trio had pitched marbles with Sonny boy, Atibi Boolitan's son, and they had lost all their new crystal-target marbles to Sonnyboy in the winner-take-all game. Single handedly none could beat Sonnyboy in a fair fist fight so the Trio held Sonnyboy in a choke hold and stripped Sonnyboy of the marbles they lost, and took Sonnyboy's marbles too.

The Trio remained on the same spot below the rose mango tree that shades Lyris George's half-dirt-half-board house, divided their spoils, and continued to pitch marbles among themselves. Then a voice is heard. It was Boolitan's: "Niggers, niggers, nigger-thieves! I want back my boy's crystal marbles." The Terrible Trio dashed off and sprinted like wild horses. When Steve, the oldest-nigger thief, looked back, he hollered, "Oh gawd! Oh gawd! Tony, Reynold, let us drop all the marbles and run through the picker by the pumping jack. Boolitan has his 'coolie gun,' and the blade is shining!"

Boolitan picked up his son's marbles, and shouted, "If I did catch all you nigger thieves, your blood woulda be on my blade in Gower's

Well Road."

Gower's Well Road is a branch road off Fyzabad's main road. It is a mile and one-half long, half-way coated with asphalt. It branches off into a graveled road on the right mound where Umy James, a taciturn woman, lives; it turns left at the fork in the road where the alligators from the dam come out at nights to roam in Lyris George's half-done house which is opposite a permanent-muddy track where Leoni Sears and Elaine Trotman abide in half-done shacks; it continues right rising up a red hill by Zoffi Thakur and Miss Sammy by the rose mango tree, and finally Gower's Well Road meanders its way on the sandy track welcoming Mother Gerald, the Spiritual Baptist woman and her sister, Rose Scott, Delcina Campbell, Miss Boolitan who makes the best roti in Fyzabad, Lottie Dublin, and ends by Miss Dora, the bungalow woman.

The two main buildings on Gower's Well Road are the Fyzabad Post Office, its post mistress, Miss Jacob, and the Fyzabad market with is favorite butchers, Mark, Millette, and Patel. Equally important to the people of

Gower's Well Road and its environs is Gower's well which is like an oasis in the desert in the dry season. When there is no water in the County Council's roadside pipes or the water on City Council's trucks ceases to come, the inhabitants walk with their ropes tied to their buckets to let down into the well for water, sometimes dirty. At the well all sweeps of social movements are discussed discretely, and the gossips of the district are blared across the well. Fights occur regularly as to who came before the other. Ziffo Thakur's noises from his machete on the grinding stone are discussed at length between the Indian and Creole people. His disturbing noise in the neighborhood is one of the few things the two races agree on.

Madam Joe uses the grinding noise as a clock alarm at 4 a.m. to get up to cook for her husband, Joseph Sears, and her sons, Paul and Alex. Joseph worked in Vessigny, a long distance from Fyzabad; and he rode to work on his Raleigh bicycle. Paul, fifteen, a welder, rode to work at TLL (Trinidad Leasehold Limited) oilfields. Alex left home last. He took the TGR (Trinidad Government Railway) bus to school in San Fernando. Madam Joe was finished cooking. She dished out Joseph and Paul's lunch, packed their bags, and they rode off to work. Behind their backs they could still hear in the distance the grinding sound that came from Ziffo Thakur's blade on the red hill above Madam Joe's unfinished board house, thatched with leaves.

Alex was with the usual crowd waiting on the TGR bus in front of Sin Kin shop. The bus was never on time to take the children to their high schools and colleges in San Fernando. The Convent girls, the Naparima girls, the Naparima boys, the Presentation boys, and the Oxford Commercial College boys and girls crowded the front of Sin Kin shop that sold home-made delicacies.

Madam Joe came running with Alex's lunch. Alex had packed his book bag in his bedroom and forgot to pick up his lunch on the kitchen counter. Madam Joe's footsteps and her backside were in competition with each other rushing to meet Alex before the TGR bus comes. But all Norris Bobcome's eyes saw was Madam Joe's derrière as it moved up and down.

Norris shouted: "All you, all you, look at how that woman's backside is jumping up and down like a see-saw." He shouted consecutively.

Nobody acknowledged his cries.

He shouted louder.

The Convent and Naparima High School girls invented time to straighten the pleats on their skirts. Straightening their pleats was like "painting the lily." Their starched pleats didn't need straightening. But the girls had to do something to pretend that they did not hear Norris' vulgar cries. The boys ran into Sin Kin shop and purchased tamarind balls. Only Mankong Lumkam remained outside. He spoke in Norris' ear. "That woman is Alex's mother."

"What! What! That's Alex's mother for true?"

"Yes, Norris," Mankong said with a broad smile.

The arriving bus saved the morning of the students' lingering embarrassment. Norris rushed into the bus. He forgot his gentleman's way of letting the girls board the bus first. For the ten miles from Fyzabad to San Fernando, Norris faked sleeping to prevent looking into Alex's face. He stopped taking the bus in front of Sin Kin shop.

When Alex returned from school, he related his Mother how Norris described her backside. She laughed for five minutes, but the noise from Ziffo Thakur's grinding stone drowned her laughter.

"Mother, I know why Ziffo is sharpening his coolie gun."

"Keep your knowledge to yourself. How many times do I have to tell you not to call neighbor Thakur a coolie. I don't like when Indian people call me a nigger."

It was the beginning of December and there were other noises in the still of the night. The big boys were bursting bamboo, and the little boys were bursting carbide packed into tins. Those games were dangerous pastimes but that was what the boys of Fyzabad had for fun. The children were learning carols. In Alex's house, his Father killed a pig and shared it with the neighbors. Madam Joe made sure the entrails of the pig were hers to make blood pudding. She had a cottage industry with the sale of blood pudding.

To Alex, there was no place in the world greater than Fyzabad. He admired the drilling wells near his house. He loved to see the men climb the derricks. As dangerous as it was, and he knew one of his schoolmates, Kenneth Dixon, lost his leg riding on the pumping jack, he too rode the pumping jack. The grinding noises from Thakur's machete gave him a new way of hugging the pumping jack. When the pumping jack came down he jumped off. Kenneth Dixon lost his leg because he jumped off when the pumping jack went up.

When the merry-go-round came to Fyzabad was another highlight of the district. Alex would do all his chores to get ten cents for five penny rides on the wooden horses, and he'd show his skill of balancing on the horses. He stood on one leg as the horses go up and down, round and round. He knew where the watchman was, and he would sit on the horse when he came near to the watchman. The watchman knew he was a brat, and refused to take his penny sometimes.

Fyzabad's biggest sports meet was climbing the greasy pole, and the winner was always an Indian boy named Chatoor. In the history of the sports, once a Creole boy, nicknamed by the Indians the "Nigger Champ," won, and the Creole people celebrated the victory of the Nigger Champ as if Jesus Christ had come to rejoice and drink kakapool (cheap rum) with them.

A new day had come and all the rollicking and merriment times came to an end, but not the grinding sound of Zoffi Thakur's machete on the grinding stone.

Alex opened the conversation. "Mother, I know why Thakur is grinding his machete. I heard him speaking in Hindi to Boolitan that his wife gets love letters from a nigger man, and that nigger man's blood will be on his machete blade. And Boolitan was telling Thakur niggers are thieves, and they smell stink. They don't know that I can speak and understand Hindi."

"Alex, it's time to go to bed. You have to get up early to catch your bus for school tomorrow." She pretended she didn't care to listen to him, but when she woke him up for school, she said, "Alex, do you know the nigger man that Thakur and Boolitan were speaking about?"

"They didn't call his name for me to hear."

Alex was dressed for school, and Madam Joe made sure he picked up the brown paper bag with his lunch. She filled the tub with rain water and threw all the men's clothes in it. She rubbed her husband's blue docks with blue soap and scrubbed them with all her strength to remove the oil marks. She repeated the rubbing and scrubbing constantly until the oil marks disappeared, and then she rinsed the four pants. She spent an hour washing all the male clothes. Then she rested on the bench and thought of what Alex said. Her thoughts asked, "Who could that nigger man be?"

She went back, washed the balance of the clothes, and emptied the tub. She filled it with rain water and had a bath. She was satisfied with how she spent her day. Now it was time to make dinner. But somehow she had a judgmental stare at her husband as he walked in.

"How was your day, Madam Joe?" he asked.

"Fine, Joseph. I washed today, and cooked for you and the boys."

"How come? Today is not Thursday, your washing day. Why did you wash today?"

"To tell you the truth, I do not know why."

"You always line up your ducks: Sunday is for cooking crab and callaloo; Monday is for mending our clothes; Tuesday is for listening to Paul talking about his welding trade as an apprentice; Wednesday is for smelling Alex's arms to see if his perspiration is talking to Boolitan; Thursday is your washing day. Today is Friday. This is not your washing day. This is your prayer meeting day when you read the Bible. I was expecting to hear about one of the women in the Bible, and the strength of women in general. Tell me why you shifted the ducks and washed today?"

She shocked him with her question. "Joseph, you ever wrote a love letter to any one?"

He thought for a minute. "Of course, I wrote a love letter to you."

"That was many years ago. I'm speaking about recently...now?"

"Madam Joe, we'd speak after I shower and change my oily clothes."

"You and Ziffo's wife speak?"

"Yes; but I don't know the difference between her and her twin sister. I met her in the market last week, and I helped her bring her basket to her door step."

"You took her basket inside her house?"

"Me go into her house? Her husband is always sharpening his coolie gun."

"Joseph, did you go in?" She emphasized her words.

"No. And did you fill up the tub with warm water for me to bathe?"

"Joseph, I may forget my duty to Paul and Alex, my children, but I never forget my duty to my husband."

"Don't peep at me when I'm in the tub."

"I don't have to peep, Joseph. I know the size of it."

"Tonight I want you to measure it."

"Not tonight. My mind will be on the nigger man that Ziffo Thakur has in mind to kill."

Paul and Alex came crashing into the house after racing from the main road, and shouted, "Mother, is dinner ready? We are hungry."

The family had dinner. Paul talked about how his skill is improving in arc welding, and his foreman, Oudit Mungal, an Indian man, compliments him for learning the art of arc welding so quickly. Joseph looked at Alex and asked, "Do you still speak Hindi?"

"When I speak it to Indian people, they pretend they do not know what I say. Now, I do not speak to them in Hindi. I only listen as if I don't know what they are saying."

Joseph said, "Alex, tell me something that you heard."

"I heard neighbor Thakur telling Boolitan in Hindi that he's going to kill a nigger."

"Why?" his Mother asked.

"Because he found a letter that his wife, Rena, got from a nigger."

"Did he talk in Hindi how he knew it was from a nigger?"

"They were looking at me, so I kept walking fast. I didn't know whether he said who."

"Paul and Alex, go and fill the tub and have your bath. I want to talk to your Father who is always saying how Rena is a pretty Indian woman. Your Father forgot Rena was barely a teenager when she came here married under bamboo with all the Hindu rites."

# 2

All Madam Joe's days were routine. At 4 a.m. she was in the kitchen cooking for her husband and children. At six, she packed their lunch bags. But somehow she was not friendly with Joseph for many days. When he jumped on his bicycle, he said, "See you later, alligator."

She did not answer her usual, "Be careful crossing the road, crocodile."

He shouted, "I told you the gospel truth last night, Madam Joe."

Paul said, "Mother, what truth Father told you last night?"

"He lied his ass out."

"But you told Alex and me you married Jo-

seph because in your two years of courtship before marriage he never lied to you. Why would
he lie to you now?" He didn't wait for an answer. He rode off on his Raleigh bicycle to work
at Forest Reserve.

Alex walked into the kitchen to get his
lunch for school and said, "Good morning,
Mother."

"Good morning. Repeat what else you
heard Zoffi Thakur telling Boolitan in Hindi."

"He said he's going to cut off his wife's neck,
and he's going to cut off the neck of the nigger
who is writing Rena letters; and then he'll kill
himself."

"Did he say who is the nigger?"

"I kept walking because I did not want
them to know I was listening to their conversation."

"Alex, don't forget your lunch today."

"No, Mother. Norris hides from me, and
he doesn't take the bus by Sin Kin shop again."

"Boys will be boys. He didn't lie on my
backside. He told the truth. I cannot prevent
my backside from jumping up and down like the
see-saw when I walk. God gave me that back-

side. Why did you come home so late yesterday?"

"The creek mile which is the short cut between San Fernando and Fyzabad was flooded; and the TGR bus had to go through Debe and Penal to get to Fyzabad."

As soon as Alex left, she heard the bell on the gate. "It's you, neighbor Zoffi?"

"Yes, Madam Joe."

"Come in."

"Can I sit on your bench while you wash?"

"Sure."

"Since I'm living here, this is the first time you walk in the short cut through the garden and come by me. Rena always walks through the short cut and comes and chats with me."

"Rena never told me that she comes by you, regularly."

"Not regularly, now and then. Why are you always making noise sharpening your machete on that grinding stone and preventing me from sleeping at nights?" She kept scrubbing her clothes on the scrubbing board.

"Madam Joe, look here."

She stopped scrubbing and looked at what

he was pointing to. "Is that blood on your machete?"

"Yes, Madam Joe. That's my blood on the blade."

"You got cut when you were brushing the bush in your vegetable garden?"

"I put my blood there. And the next blood will not be mine."

She was about to ask Thakur: Whose blood it would be? But a sudden shower came down. She rushed and picked up her clothes from the line; he ran quickly through the short cut, and picked up the shelled corn that he had drying on a sheet of galvanized iron in the sun.

Madam Joe couldn't wait to tell her husband what was on her mind. As Joseph jumped off his bicycle, she took the bicycle from his hand, parked it below the house, and said, "I want to talk to you now."

"Why now? I worked on the derrick; I was in oil; and we capped a flowing well today."

"Okay. But we must discuss what is on my mind after you bathe in the tub."

The tone of her voice awakened the culture of their courtship when she dressed and waited for him when the Apex Oilfield whistle blew and signaled the close of day for the oilfield workers. He had worked for Apex until the strike led by the one-man trade union, Tubal Uriah Butler. He was never a Butlerite but the police came looking for him when Charlie King was burned to death. A police informer had described him as a man on the scene of Charlie King's murder.

The other culture of the Sears family was to buy a bottle of cherry brandy wine on June 19 to celebrate Butler Day, and talk about the greatness of Butler. Joseph thought his wife was again going to probe him to know if he were there when Charlie King was burned to death. She never believed he was not there. But her topic surprised him.

"Joseph, I'm anxious to hear of your friendship with Thakur's wife, and how you write poetry to her like this one: I am Creole/ You are Indian/ Let us sow our seed in one pod."

He was out of the wooden tub enclosed with canvas. "Madam Joe, where did you find that?"

"When I emptied the tub, it was wet, and I dried it by the coal pot."

"Woman, I don't feel like talking tonight. I had a tough day at work. Go in my pocket and you'll find money to shop for Christmas. Christmas is just one week away."

Fyzabad's women have the biggest falling out with their husbands, boyfriends, or common law companions come Christmas time. The women see both sides of "now," and know the side the man will choose to share his meager salary. Most times the man has to share his salary with his wife, common law wife, and many girlfriends. Not Joseph. He was faithful to Madam Joe so letting her go into his pocket was no big deal. She calculated how much money she will need for the family of four to buy Christmas gifts, food, and new curtains.

Another culture of Fyzabad's women, second to gossip, is they hung their curtains late at nights bordering on Christmas morning because they didn't want their neighbors to know beforehand what they bought. Once Madam Joe got up and saw Lyris George had the same curtains hanging on her doors and windows blown by the Christmas breeze. Madame Joe had traveled ten miles to San Fernando to buy her curtains so nobody in Fyzabad would have the same curtains as she. Lyris George had the same thought. Lyris had traveled to San Fernando and shopped for curtains at the same store Madam Joe had shopped for curtains. Joseph laughed and teased his wife: "Madam Joe, next time go to London to buy your curtains." Joseph's laughter was their only disagreement that Christmas morn.

Not so with the other families. Their warring about money at Christmas time was constant.

The market on Gower's Well Road and the sidewalks were filled with merchants from nearby towns. The streets were filled with women spending their husbands' back-pay money from the oilfields; so too were the gossipers bad-mouthing everybody but themselves.

"Madam Joe, wait a minute," Doris called out.

"Yes, Fig Foot." That was Doris' nickname because she had a large foot because of infantile paralysis.

"I hear that coolie man, Thakur, found poems your husband wrote to his wife. I hear she likes nigger men. I also heard before Boozie went to England he carried Thakur's wife down NMC Road and they had sex by the pumping jack."

"Big Foot, what you heard about Boozie could be true; but what you heard about my husband could never be true. My husband leaves home six in the morning riding his bicycle to Vessigny which is a long distance from Fyzabad, and he comes back seven at nights. Tell me, Big Foot, when would my husband get the time to write Thakur's wife love letters?"

"Thelma who is living down by Johnny's well told me so."

"Picky-head Thelma knows everybody's business, and that's why her man left her with five children and gone to live with a young girl."

"I heard he left her because the last two Chinese-looking children are not his."

"I can't see how creole Willy could get up every morning and look at those Chinese-colored children and say they are his."

"So you don't think your husband could write those poems to that coolie woman in his lunch time when he is not climbing on the derrick?"

"Where would he get paper and pen when he has to cap them overflowing oil wells?"

"Probably it is your son, Paul, who is with Thakur's wife. I heard that coolie woman likes Paul because they are the same age; Thakur could be her father; and he has an eternal sore foot. How old is Paul now?"

"Sixteen."

Madam Joe took up her goods, walked slowly down Gower's Well Road, and lugged herself through the mud track that separated her from Elaine Trotman. On her mind was whether Paul ever took Thakur's wife down NMC Road, and if Paul is the nigger man's blood that Thakur wants on his blade. Then she spoke to herself: "Rena is a decent young woman. I knew her since she was a little girl when she married under bamboo and came to live on the hill facing us. Rena is no longer practicing Hindu customs, and when she comes by me, we talk about how she is sorry she doesn't have a baby for Zoffi; and she talks about her twin sister, Ria, who told her Father she'll run away if he insists marrying her under bamboo. Ria had told her Pa she wants to be a bookkeeper at Rahamut Stores in San

Fernando. I don't believe what people are saying about Rena. I wonder if these gossipers in Fyzabad are mistaking Ria for Rena. They are identical twins. Could be. Could be."

# 3

Paul became silent and somewhat reserved, and his Mother and Father each night prayed for him. They thought he had mental problems. Sometimes they called in Alex to kneel and pray with them for Paul. After prayers they asked Alex for his observation about Paul.

"Paul is fine, Mother. He is more than fine, Father."

"That's all?" Joseph asked. "You sleep in the same room, and on the same bed. He gives you money. He takes you to cinema...Does he still love Dorothy?"

"No."

"Why?"

"He never told me why."

To Paul, unknown to his parents, not Alex, Fyzabad would only be a place to sleep overnight after his apprenticeship is over at TLL. He would go and live in San Fernando and get a job on the port or in Neal and Massey. Then he will go and live in the City of Port of Spain when he is confident of his ability as a first class welder and become a teacher at Trinidad & Tobago Electricity Commission. It was as if the society and the culture of Fyzabad were beneath his dignity. He'd no longer hear the siren of Apex Oilfields blowing for workers to come and labor. He'd no longer hear the weeping of the wives of the lotto losers or see his brother waiting for two hours for the TGR bus in front of Sin Kin shop. Better still, he'd never hear the sound coming from Ziffo Thakur's grinding stone.

One more year and his apprenticeship would be over, and he'd be gone. He has a girl pen pal who lives alone in Petra Street, Woodbrook, Port of Spain, and he'll take her up on the invitation to share her room with her. She had told him in a letter that she is a virgin, a good Christian, and she will never have premarital sex. Paul told her in his last pen-pal letter, "Susannah, distance lends enchantment to the view. When I share the room with you, our room should have a red bulb and a green bulb. When I turn on the red bulb on Petra Street, frontiers will be distance apart; when I turn on the green bulb you may find a way of narrowing the once distant vow of chastity, and we may become physical."

She had written back: "Dear Paul, are you an apprentice welder or the son of William Shakespeare? I hope you are the son of Shakespeare. If you are, I will turn on the green bulb in our room after I shower in the bathroom that has no doors."

"Susannah, my Indian boss at TLL calls me a good Creole apprentice, and he tells me if I could weld friendship smoothly as I weld steel, I can bring people together—those who live on Petra Street in north Trinidad who think they are superior to the people in Fyzabad which is in south Trinidad. Do you believe him?"

"You'd know if I believe your boss by the color of the lit bulb after having my bath. I'd do like Rod Stewart and wait *Until the Real Thing Comes Along*."

"By the way, Susan, are you Creole or Indian?"

"When you come you'll see. The only clue I'd give you is that I wear hipsters to sleep."

The days in Paul's life passed with fits-and-starts. His hormones began raging but no longer for Susannah and the nights she'd put on the green bulbs in Petra Street to let him know she's not going to follow her vow of not having premarital sex. At nights, he'd look through his darkened southern window that faces Rena's lit northern window, and he'd see Rena changing her clothes without pulling down the blind. Then he'd look at her unplaiting her fishbone braids slowly and smiling as if she knows he's looking at her. At times he wondered if she really forgot to pull the blinds, if she left them up, purposely, for him to admire all her nocturnal movements, and he exclaimed, "Damn! Does she know what's she's doing to my body?"

Alex walked in the room and interrupted his thoughts. "What are you thinking? It is not yet June 19 to celebrate Butler Day and your birthday."

"Alex, I'm thinking of when you comprehend something, you understand what it means."

"Yes, Paul."

"But comprehend what?"

"What you understand. I want to be a poet like Mr. Telemaque." Harold M. Telemaque was the headmaster at Fyzabad Anglican School and a poet. Every Friday every student had to recite his composition in front of the class. Critiques could only be positive comments. Ria was always the best with her critiques; and she made it her duty to critique Paul's comments every Friday.

"Big brother, you want to write poems for Ziffo's wife?"

Paul remained silent for fully ten seconds before he replied. "Alex, why that question?"

"Paul, when you comprehend something, you understand what it means."

"Let's talk hormones politics, Alex."

"When I come home after school I'll discuss hormones politics. If I miss my bus this morning, I'll have to walk ten miles to San Fernando. No matter how loud the sound of the coolie gun on Ziffo's grinding stone, we'd lock the door and talk." He took up his book bag and brown paper bag with his lunch and ran as fast as possible through the muddy track by Elaine Trotman and Lyris George. He screamed to the bus driver to stop; and he jumped in.

At work, Alvin Thomas was on the lathe turning out a blade, and he said, "Paul, I want you to weld on the handle, not for me; it is for the boss."

"Sure." Paul did not ask Alvin, his adviser on women, the question on his mind. Nonetheless, he was thinking of Rena who looks beautiful in sari with her midriff exposed. They had spoken as children when she lived in Delhi Road. She, too, had gone to the Presbyterian Sunday school. Alex had told him the girls sat on the left side of the aisle and the boys sat on the right side. Alex remembered her very well and was shocked to see when she moved to the new house on the hill overlooking them. The previous owner was the Edwards, a Creole family. When a room was added to the Sears's house, Paul told his parents he wants that room, and Alex knew why. At nights Paul prevented Alex from coming into his room, and Alex suspected Rena and Paul had met secretly since their adulthood, and Alex also suspected they had patterns of shared behavior.

Alex went to bed that night, and, to him, the grinding noise from the Thakur's household never stopped until morning.

It was Madam Joe's washing day. She took water from the rain drums and filled the wooden tub. Her head bobbed forward and the strength from her arms drained the oil from Joseph's blue docks and the mud from the boys' khaki uniform. She heard the sound of the bottom of the uneven gate grating the dirt, and she knew who was at the gate. She shouted, "Neighbor Zoffi, I hope you didn't come with rain to wet up my clothes on the line again."

"I come to tell you that I have a man to kill to put his blood on my poonyah. I grind my poonyah for the whole night."

Madam Joe did not stop washing. "Neighbor, what that man did to you?"

"He would not stop writing poetry and love letters for my wife."

"What kind of man is that?" She walked away and put some clothes on the grass to bleach in the sun. Then she wiped the perspiration on her face with the bottom of her dress. "Where he lives?"

"In Gower's Well Road." He left, but he did not take the normal route by Elaine Trotman and Lyris George's houses. He walked in the mud track through Madam Joe's garden that is bounded by his garden, and when he reached his house he mumbled, "This is the way he comes to my house when I'm not here. That is why I'll never stop sharpening my machete for his nigger neck."

# 4

The Sears family sat for dinner, and having dinner together was a culture of the family. That culture was different for most Fyzabadian parents who told their children, "Do not speak when we are eating at the table because that is bad table manners." Madam Joe wanted to hear her boys speak with fervor, and she loved when they argued about who got more meat in his plate. Joseph loved to fan the flame that "a mother's first child is always her favorite child." He fans the flame higher and says, "The apprentice gives his Mother his pay envelope from TLL, and he is satisfied with the little pocket change that his Mother gives him. That little boy who still goes to school in San Fernando and wants to be a solicitor to work in Mr. Misir's office doesn't have a pay envelope to bribe his way into a certain person's heart."

Madam Joe smiled, and said, "Paul, please, say the Grace."

Paul seemed distant and disgusted with the conversation at hand. He turned the *Grace before Meal* into a sociological text of cultural relativity. "Dear Lord, Creole people in Fyzabad should love the Indian people all over the world and their love for each other should be reciprocated without bitterness, but with kindness."

Madam Joe's bent neck became erect, and she looked at Paul.

"And, dear Lord, the people around this table are few, and we are going to have a meal that thousands of Indian children will never have. Dear Lord, we who can sit at sundown and sup with our family should be grateful. I, as an individual, love Indian people. Amen."

"Paul," Joseph said but looked at Alex, "your Mother found a sheet of poetry when she emptied the tub. Was it yours?"

"I hate poetry! I never understand what

poets write. To me, they are all sissies," Alex blurted.

"I'm addressing the favorite son," Joseph said.

"I have batches of your poems, Father," Paul answered.

Madam Joe said, "Paul, do you know where to find your Father's poems?"

"Sure!"

"Bring them to me. After dessert there'll be poetry reading by the bard of Gowers Well Road."

In a family there is always an equal opportunity offender. That part of the personality that is unconscious and represents instinctual needs and drives is aligned to Paul. That part of the personality responsible for conscious decision making falls in the arms of Alex. That part of the personality that represents socially accepted values relates to Madam Joe. She is the conscience—her own, and thinks other's conscience should be akin to hers. Joseph's conscience was like the weather cock's which moved with the wind.

Madam Joe demanded Joseph to sit down

and read the poems he wrote that Paul is in love with. He refused.

"Then, my dear husband, I will read them." She began: "Indians lay down your ridicule of us. /You call us niggers without provocation, sometimes /Creole people do the same/ Indians, you were paid for your labor/ You were advised by the Indian Commissioner who came from India/ We have our local Commissioner, Creole Butler, our earthly savior."

She read another poem: "My hobby is climbing derricks/ Way on top the derricks/You down there are tiny to me/ I up here am tiny to you/ We are the same with relativity."

She read the last poem: "I love Indian movies/ I love the way Indian women dance with vulgarity and virtue in their hips/ And I sin when I watch/ The only thing I hate about Indian movies/ Are the scenery about nature/That come on the screen when lovers are in bed/ I had an Indian lover/ And I lost her to prejudice."

The whistling sound of the kettle sent steam out that blasted the wall, and Madam Joe made a sign to Joseph to stay in his seat, and he obeyed knowing the wrath of hell will be his reward if he disobeyed. She walked slowly and turned off the fire under the kettle. The handle of the kettle was soldered on by Paul when he began learning the welding trade and even though Joseph bought a new kettle she preferred to use the kettle Paul soldered. She walked slowly back to the table and Joseph spoke of going into his garden to cut a juicy sugar cane to distract her thoughts from discussions on his poems. Poor try, Joseph.

Madam Joe read a line in his poem and said, "Joe, you never told me you lost your Indian lover to prejudice?"

Alex shouted: "Was she pretty as Rena, Father?" He ran from the table.

"You had sex with her?" Paul ran from the table too.

Madam Joe said, "Why not answer your boys' questions? They are beyond the age of puberty."

Joseph answered. "She was prettier than Rena, and we had good times."

"In bed?" Madam Joe asked, and did not get an answer.

"You read poetry to her in bed, Father?" Alex shouted, and he did not get an answer.

Madam Joe smiled. "Joseph, lying to your children is a sin. Let them know some of your experiences with women so they will learn from you a thing or two from their poetic Father who loves women with long hair, and thick gold bracelets and gold chains hanging from their necks."

"Madam Joe, I knew Paul loved Rena from the day she moved into that house above us. I knew she was fond of him but held her fondness to herself because she was a new bride. And I know she comes and chats with you, and she will never tell Thakur that she comes through the mud track to come to your house. That blade that Thakur is sharpening is for a nigger's blood. That nigger is your first born."

"That nigger could be you because Thakur can say you encourage your son to be with his wife because his cousin jilted you. You never stopped loving that Indian woman who jilted you; and your boys have your genes. Both of them told me they go to Indian movies. Last week they saw *Doly* at Ideal Theatre, and they discussed the movie with you."

The wisdom of Madam Joe became a thesis

statement to the men folks who live in the end of the mud track in Gower's Well Road.

"One of the men in my house is in love with Thakur's wife," she said to herself, as she rubbed blue soap on three pants at the same time. That grip on three pants at the same time is an acquired art. Then she separated the clothes and put Alex's pants only on the scrubbing board and pushed a corn husk with vigor on the pockets and knees of his pants. Then she spoke to the pants. "Alex, I sent you from age eight to the Presbyterian Sunday school to learn Hindi and to get some of Padma Kumari's teachings of Christianity, and not to covet what the Indian children have because the Creole children have good things too." She took that pants and put it to bleach on the grass. She looked up in the sky and said, "I hope no rain comes today."

She repeated the same washing movements for Joseph's pants, but said, "You never told me you had a coolie woman with long hair before you had me, the nigger woman, with picky hair." She walked to the grass, looked up in the sky again, and said, "The sky is blue. The sun is shining and your blue docks will get the sun in your crotch." She rested Joseph's pants next to Alex's.

Paul's pants got her full strength. It seems that she always has more feelings for whatever concerns Paul—his trade, his intelligence, his good looks, his manners for Elaine, the Shango-Baptist neighbor, and the Grenadian neighbor, Lyris, who lives on the edge of the dam and was always chasing alligators from her yard. Lyris called Paul so often to chase alligators from her yard that she paid him ten cents for each alligator he pushed back into the dam. Just as she was about to put Paul's pants to bleach next to the others, the bell rang on the rusty gate. It was Zoffi Thakur. She said a silent prayer to God to teach her diplomacy to handle Satan. Zoffi was her Satan. "And only Satan would want to kill my first born."

"Neighbor Zoffi, come sit on the bench and talk while I knock out this last pants. Your sore foot healed as yet?" He didn't answer her question.

"Madam Joe, how long you are living here in Gower's Well Road?"

"About two years after neighbor Lyris George."

"You know she was mad."

She ignored his statement. "Last week was forty years I'm living in this old house. All my children were born here. When I came to live here almost the whole of Gower's Well Road was bush, bush, everywhere. By the way, all through the night I heard you sharpening your machete. Why do you sharpen it so often on that grinding stone?"

"Madam Joe, before I die, I have a man to kill."

She changed the conversation from a crime topic to what happens on a sunny day. "Thakur, I'm trying to catch the sun before God takes it away from me."

"Madam Joe, whose pants you just put on the bleach to catch the sun?"

"Alex's." She lied.

"Rena told me she and Alex went to the Presbyterian Sunday school when they were children, and then they went to the Anglican school when Mr. Telemaque was the head teacher."

"Alex never told me a thing about that."

"Never?"

"Never!" She lied.

"Do they talk to each other?"

"Not since you married Rena under bamboo."

"Before that?"

"I guess so. Teenagers do not discuss their lives with their parents."

He took out his machete from the case on his waist.

"Thakur, why do you walk with your gillpin when you come to chat with me?"

"I want to cut one of your sugar canes to suck."

"Go and cut as many as you wish. When your dasheen bush grows taller, I will come and cut some."

Effortlessly, the wind from his blade swiped the root and leaves off the sugar cane. He looked at Madam Joe and said, "You see how sharp my coolie gun is?"

He went away sucking his cane, and she went inside and anxiously awaited the arrival of her husband who came minutes later.

"Joseph, Thakur came to see me today?"

"For what, Madam Joe?"

"To chat."

"About his sore foot that wouldn't heal?"

"That too."

"No young woman likes being with an old man whose sore smells."

Madam Joe looked at her sons around the dinner table. "Do you think it is right for a woman to stay with her husband if he has a sore foot that smells?"

None of her sons answered. She again turned her questions to Joseph. "Joseph, Rena told you that?"

"No."

"Then how do you know Thakur's sore smells?"

"The chief culture of Fyzabad is gossip."

Madam Joe filled four glasses of lime squash. She handed Paul a glass and said, "Paul and Alex, I suspect both of you look at Rena from your window at nights."

They did not answer.

"Did you hear what I said?"

Both denied.

"Thakur said his wife told him so. After Thakur cut the cane he walked to his house by walking in the grass straight to his house. He was counting the amount of footsteps from our window to his wife's window. If he comes to talk with me tomorrow I will ask him why he was doing that."

Paul said, "Mother, next week Monday do not get up early to cook for me. The company will be having a ceremony for the end of my apprenticeship. I expect to see my Father in his serge suit after he puts it in the sun and he brushes last year's dust off; and my Mother should be wearing her corset with her dress."

"How many of you will be graduating?"

"Twenty Five."

"What's your trade?" She smiled.

"Acetylene and arc welding."

"The kettle you soldered is still good. Do you still love nosy me?"

"That's one thing I wouldn't change my mind about."

"Your Father used those same words when I asked him if he still loves me."

"Goodnight, Mother."

"Good night, Paul. Abstain tonight from looking at the window on the hill."

"I'll do whatever you say, Mother, to please

you. But other males look at the window on the hill, I assure you."

# 5

Leoni Sears was born Leoni Albertina Samuel in Mason Hall, Tobago, in 1908 to a Mother who was a farmer, and a Father who was an overseer in the Road Works of the County Council. Her Father did not live with her Mother, and although she saw her Father periodically she did not know his address. Little Lo, as she was called, learned the culture and survival instincts of Mothers without money who survived without a male in the house. She had concerns against her own childhood. But her concerns bridged a gap of the fear of hunger and the fear that she may become a thief if there was no money to be had before her Mother's crops are harvested. She had told Paul and Alex how she survived in Tobago when she was seven, and she called the name of the man who knew she was stealing his eggs as soon as the hens laid. In fact, she told Paul and Alex the whole story when their Father was not around.

Papa Lee made it easy for her to stop stealing his eggs. He gave her two laying hens as an Easter gift. Easter Sunday was a big festive holiday in Tobago. There were crab race and goat race, and the Moravian Church had their harvest. The Minister opened the harvest with a speech of commendation. He said: "Leoni Samuel, whom we lovingly know as Little Lo, brought three dozen eggs; the cooks cooked one dozen; and there are two dozen remaining for sale. The sale from the two dozen eggs will be for the new altar of this church. Little Lo told me old Papa Lee, a wise man, gave her two laying hens last year that lay golden eggs. I am sure Papa Lee saw the honesty in Little Lo. Let us pray for Little Lo because her gift came from her honest hand."

Easter Monday in Tobago came to mind when Madam Joe stirred her pot of callaloo. But now in Fyzabad, Madam Joe's happiness depended on finding out which one of the men in her house is in danger. She knew before the day is over Ziffo Thakur will be pushing her gate, and the bell will ring to announce his arrival with his machete at his side in a leather case. With the many arrays of her worldly experience, her intuition that moment told her Thakur will be coming to tell her or to torture her of whose Creole blood would be on his machete.

The bell rang and it completely knocked out the thoughts that she was a little thief and Papa Lee read her intentions whenever she dropped by to sweep the sand under his house where the hens laid their eggs.

"Madam Joe, good morning."

"Good morning, neighbor Thakur. Thanks for your callaloo bush."

"I didn't come with my poonyah today."

"Why, neighbor Thakur?"

"I didn't sharpen it last night, and the blade looks rusty. I oiled it down with cooking oil and left it leaning on the grinding stone."

"You look odd without that poonyah on your side."

"You know what I come to talk to you

about?"

"No."

"I'm hearing a rumor."

"What kind of rumor?" Madam Joe knew she stepped out on faith with that question. She pulled the bench closer to the tub and told him to sit. She began to wash light clothes and took the corn husk from the hole in the scrubbing board and scrubbed with vigor. He knew her next move, and he did the needful.

"Madam Joe, let me dip out water from the drum with rain water for you to rinse the clothes."

"Thank you." She was afraid to ask him about the rumor he heard. "I hope you didn't bring rain today."

"I left my machete home today so rain will not come." Both of them laughed heartily.

She found courage and asked. "What is the rumor you come to tell me?"

"It is not a rumor: You can cut as much dasheen bush as you want."

"Neighbor, do you know what we Creole people say when we cook dasheen and dasheen bush?"

"No."

"We say we are eating 'on top and below' because the dasheen bush grows on top the tree, and the dasheen fruit grows in the ground." They chuckled.

"Madam Joe, can you lend me your machete to cut a cane?"

"Remember my poonyah is not as sharp as yours."

"I have a dull poonyah home that I use to cut off a fowl's neck whenever Rena wants a fowl to cook. How many canes I can cut?"

"As many as you wish."

She could not wait for the four diners to sit around the table to discuss Thakur's visit without his poonyah at his side.

"Do you believe he came to tell you that you can pick callaloo bush?" Joseph asked.

"Joseph, your guess is as good as mine."

"Why he left his machete home? Is he no longer going to put a creole's blood on his blade?"

Alex said, "It will not be my blood because the girl I dreamed of since I was in Sunday school sits on my lap in the TGR bus, and her culture is not her parents.'"

Paul shouted, "She speaks to you in Hindi?"

"For sure. She will not be attending your apprenticeship graduation."

Their mother listened to their discussion but said nothing. Nonetheless, her reflection of an incident of the recent past was vivid in her mind. Only a week ago an Indian man had killed his wife and hung himself. Alex and other children had dropped out of their bus on their way home from school and had gone to see the suicidal Indian man who was hanging from a short piece of rope. The rumor was "a nigger man was boning his wife." Somehow Madam Joe worked up the energy to talk to her sons about cultural relativity—judging another culture objectively—and spoke in plain language to drive home the point why neighbors should not use the words Nigger and Coolie to address each other. But at the same time she wanted to know if her boys had stepped out of their race to find Indian girlfriends. Her way of finding out was by way of hygiene.

"Alex, your perspiration is talking. Make sure you wash your arms with baking soda to kill that smell because Indian people say Creole people smell bad." She looked at him. "Is she Creole or Indian?"

"Didn't you hear when your first born asked me if she speaks Hindi, and I said yes."

"I was not listening to your conversation."

"Aren't you going to ask your first born if his choice is Coolie or Nigger?"

"I just spoke to you about those distasteful words, and that you must judge people the way you want them to judge you." She hummed in the style of Deanna Durbin singing *Night and Day*. Paul hummed with his Mother and picked up his banjo. They watched Alex as he walked out with his brown lunch bag and his satchel on his back as he raced to get the TGR bus.

# 6

All the proud parents and friends of the graduating apprentices were having a rollicking time at the party held in Forest Reserve Senior Staff Clubhouse. In attendance were Henry Blacksburg, the General Manager of Trinidad Leasehold Limited, and his wife, a wizened-face-looking woman in a short dress and an unruly head of hair; Wilfred D. Best, the headmaster of Forest Reserve English Catholic School, and his wife; Beryl Price, Paul's kindergarten teacher; Oudit Mungal, the head instructor of the apprentices; Joseph Sears; Leoni Sears; John Jules; Jonathan "Boozy" Valley; Steve Crooks; Reynold James; Anthony George; Lloyd

Mason; Lyris George; Elaine Trotman; Sonnyboy Bollitan; Ulric "Boong" Dublin; Fitz Fraser; Edward Noble; Austin "Skylark" Tuitt; Daniel Lewis; Kenneth Lewis; Juliet Lewis: Alvin Thomas; Kenwyn Joseph; and countless other friends and family members of the apprentices.

Ten minutes later a guest dressed in a burka, probably an Arab woman, walked in unaccompanied and left her chauffeurs, Roy and Windell, the richest Indian family in Fyzabad, waiting for her in a new Studebaker.

That guest in burka, only her eyes were seen. The only part of her attire that was known to everyone was the silk cloth that covered her body. She sat in a chair by herself, probably by design. No one knew why, and her beverage of choice was grapefruit juice. A waiter attempted to refill her half-empty glass, and she covered the top of her glass with her fingers. Her figures were beautifully manicured with clear nail polish.

Parents were congratulating each other: "My son, Henry, is a machinist and did a lot of designs on the lathe." "My boy, Jeffrey, is a pipefitter, and my husband doesn't have cause for complaints again because Jeffrey fixes all the leaks in the house." "It is so nice to see you Harriet. What your son did?" "He is now a qualified mechanic. He can fix an old engine and have it humming like the new Studebaker parked outside."

"Gina Lewis, who the hell is that woman who is hiding her face in all that cloth?" "Dorothy, ask me about my son, Coleridge. He studied with Mr. Mungal, and he is a first class electrician. Sometimes Coleridge gets fresh and says, 'Coolie Mungal is so tough on me.' I tell him, I don't want to hear him call his instructor a coolie again, because of Mr. Mungal he can earn a decent living. He and his cousin, Paul Sears, will be going to Port of Spain to look for work at Trinidad & Tobago Electricity Commission."

"Attention, everyone," Henry Blacksburg said. "Today is the graduating Class of 1952, and the fifteen apprentices in their overall uniforms will be performing for you today without tapping shoes like Rochester and Shirley Temple that you see in the movies at Ideal Theater or in carnival costumes but with their tools of choice. Each will come forward and show you his skill."

Each apprentice displayed his skill and was applauded. When Paul Sears's name was called, his Mother shouted, "Show them, my first born, all of your skills." Paul displayed his skills in acetylene and arc welding and made a pipe stove in fifteen minutes. He was wildly applauded. The woman dressed in the burka looked in Paul's direction, did not applaud, but bowed appreciatively, and left. Paul's stairs followed her to her transport. She looked at Paul, entered the Studebaker, and she left.

The parents forgot about their sons' achievements and chatted about that strange woman who came to Forest Reserve Senior Staff Club.

"Who's she?"

"Don't ask me. Ask the Manager of TLL if he invited her."

"Did she come to see Oudit Mungal?"

"I don't think so."

"Did she come to see Basdeo, the boy who is an ace mechanic?"

"Why she hid her face in this hot sun?"

"That is how Muslim women dress in Egypt."

"To me, they only dress so in this country when they marry under bamboo."

"I will make it my business and go and see Roy and Windell at their big house in Delhi Road and ask them who is the woman that they brought to Forest Reserve to see my son graduate as a motor mechanic."

The inquisitiveness and the insensitivity of that parent riled Madam Joe's sensitivity, and she spoke.

"Why are you making that woman's presence so much your business?"

"I hate Coolie people!"

"Mr. Mungal is an Indian, and he was your son's instructor. He never called your son a dunce Nigger. All he did was to give your son knowledge. Did you see how your son shook his hand with gratitude?" Madam Joe walked away, and she mumbled, "Ingratitude is worse than witchcraft."

Alex was inside doing his homework and waiting for Paul and his parents to come home. The bell on the crooked gate rang and he rushed outside. "Paul, how did it go?"

His Mother answered. "There was a beautiful Indian woman who came to see the show."

"Mother, I'm talking to Paul."

Paul took out the stove from a crocus bag and rested it on the table.

"I like it! I like it!" Alex said. "How long it took you to design and weld it?"

"Not long. I had that design in my head for months."

"Are you going to mount it up in the kitchen?"

Madam Joe answered. "That's a gift for someone."

"Mother, how do you know?" Alex said.

"I have a great suspicion that your brother will be moving out soon to live somewhere unknown to his Father and me."

"Is that so, Paul?" Alex asked with astonishment.

"I'm thinking of it," Paul answered.

"Where to?" Alex looked at him.

"To San Fernando or Port of Spain."

"So I can move into your room?"

"I did not say tomorrow."

Joseph spoke. "Madam Joe, who was that mystery woman?"

"Why not ask the graduating welder who will soon be leaving Fyzabad to live elsewhere. For one thing: soon Thakur's machete will not have his blood?"

Joseph spoke again. "Paul who is she?"

"I don't know."

"But she left after your ingenious display, and she bowed graciously after your exhibition."

"I did not notice that."

"But your eyes followed her to the Studebaker that was waiting for her."

"Other people's eyes did the same."

Madam Joe cooked a quick pot so that she could continue the conversation. She cooked rice and corned beef. She went to the back of the house and picked two sour lemons and made lemonade.

"Alex, I want you to say the *Grace before Meal*, and thank God in advance for letting your brother get a job out of Fyzabad so that you can get his bedroom," Madam Joe said.

"God, my name is Alex Sears. You already know my need. Amen."

"Paul, your turn," Madam Joe said.

He looked at his Mother and smiled.

"Thank you, God, for giving me the knowledge to graduate in my trade in five years as a damn good welder. Soon I will be applying for a job as an instructor at the Trinidad & Tobago Electricity Commission in Port of Spain. And thank you, God, for this meal. When I was small Father told Alex and me it is only lazy women who love to cook rice and corned beef in a can." He looked at his Father, and his Father was stifling his laughter. "And, God, I thank you for my little brother who wants me to move out to get my room. One more thing, Lord: I love East Indian people. But not anyone who lives in Gower's Well Road. Amen."

His Mother added. "You forgot to thank God for the woman in the burka - that loose garment covering her entire body and having only a veiled opening for eyes."

"Which woman?" Alex shouted with his mouth full of food.

"When you move into your brother's room you will have the opportunity to peep at her, uninterrupted."

"Mother, Paul is not moving out tomorrow."

Joseph spoke. "Little Lo, you are taking your imagination a bit too far. Did you hot water to throw in the tub for me to have my bath?"

"Yes, Massa sir."

"Paul, I am so proud of you. I was moved by the way your welding exhibition went. What I liked best was the way you spoke to your audience and told them about your trade as if you are already an instructor."

"Thank you, Father."

Madam Joe spoke. "Today, I, Madam Joe, am called by my baptismal name, Leoni Samuel. I am informed that I am a lazy woman because I cooked rice and corned beef in a can. But that's okay. When I was a little girl in Tobago I was the happiest kid when my Mother cooked rice and corned beef in a can. Like Oliver Twist, I always asked my Mother for more. You, highfalutin people, are bad mouthing the dish I rushed home to cook to kill your hunger." She looked at Paul. "Paul, my first born, I could not help looking at the woman in that black burka. I could not see her eyes under her veil but the angle of her head never shifted when you spoke. I, too, am proud of you. I will miss you very much when you leave to go to Port of Spain, but I want you to know for the five years that you gave me your envelope of $15.32 bi-weekly, all the money I took is in the drawer that I kept locked. Tell me the day that you are leaving, and I will hand you your money. Excuse me, gentlemen." She left the table and hot water in the kettle that Paul soldered when he was learning trade. She poured hot water in the tub, and said, "Joseph Sears, your obedient servant has just poured the hot water you demanded of her. Do you want me to go and look for your Baytee (an unmarried Indian girl) to dry your body with her long hair?"

# 7

It was Thursday, her washing day. Joseph had gone to work; Paul was having his breakfast upstairs; and Alex was about to leave to catch the TGR bus. She called Alex and gave him a lecture. "Boy, I want you to stick to your books and graduate as your brother. Doris told me that that Indian girl is always sitting on your lap in the bus. Is she an invalid?"

"Mother, how does Miss Doris know that? She doesn't travel on the bus."

"Is it true?"

"That Indian girl has a name! Did Miss Doris tell you her name?"

"I did not ask her. And I don't want you to

shout at me when I'm speaking to you. Paul has never shouted at me when I spoke to him about any woman. I want to be proud of you on your graduation day just as I was proud of Paul yesterday. Yesterday was a red-letter day for me. It is a day I will remember for a long time. I watched your brother with enormous pride when he shook Mr. Henry Blacksburg's hand. He is the General Manager of Trinidad Leasehold Limited. He told Paul he hopes he returns to work with the company."

"Mother, can you boast about your first born's sterling qualities tonight? I don't want to miss that 7.30 bus this morning. The last time I missed the bus, I had to stay home and listen to Zoffi's machete on his grinding stone for the whole day."

"And I don't want you to miss the 4 o'clock bus this afternoon to hear the excuse you will be giving me for your lateness home. Run along."

She went and got the dipper and put water in the tub. She laughed and said, "I'm going to wash Massa's clothes. He was so proud of his son yesterday." The gate was pushed and the bell rang. "My god! What is he coming to tell me today? God give me wisdom today as you gave Moses."

"Madam Joe, good morning."

"Is that you, neighbor Zoffi? These days you are scarce as hens' teeth."

"I was by my uncle in Marabella for some days. His daughter married under bamboo with all the Hindu rites. My wife was with me but she came down with Roy and Windell on Wednesday. I am sorry I did not come down with her because after she left the creek flooded, and it was very dangerous for the taxis to drive through that one mile of sea water. I cannot swim; so I remained till the water went down."

"You know Roy and Windell?"

"Their Mother and my Grandfather are siblings, and wherever they go they are dressed up."

"So you and Rena were dressed up at the wedding."

"I wasn't dressed up, but Rena was."

"How she was dressed up?"

"Nice like when she was my *dulahin*(married wife) on the day of our marriage."

"So she covered her face like when both of

you got married under bamboo?"

"I don't know why she did that."

"She changed her clothes to come home?"

"No."

"You were away, and that is why I didn't hear you grinding your poonyah?"

"But I carried it with me to Marabella because my uncle has a sharper grinding stone up there."

"Did you tell your uncle why you are sharpening your poonyah every day?"

"I told him, and he talked to Rena."

"What he told Rena?"

"Whatever he told Rena, Rena said I'm a liar; and I'm imagining things."

"And you believed Rena?" She felt she should not ask him that question, and she suddenly changed to, "Neighbor Thakur, could you dip some water and fill the tub while I go upstairs to watch my pot." She went upstairs to make sure Paul was quietly listening. He was, and she ran back downstairs. "Neighbor, you are always on time to help me, but I hope you will not bring rain with you today." When she looked at him, she did not think it was wise to repeat her last question. She said, "Neighbor, go and cut two canes."

"I don't feel like sucking cane today." He said, "Neighbor, how old is your big boy?"

"Twenty."

"He is still learning trade at TLL?"

"No."

"What is he doing now?"

"He is getting ready to go to Port of Spain to look for a job."

"What about the one who used to go to the Presbyterian Church Sunday school?"

"He goes to school in San Fernando. He wants to be a solicitor."

"Did he ever learn to speak Hindi?"

"That lazy boy didn't learn one word."

"One day Boolitan and I were speaking, and he was walking very slowly while we were speaking in our language."

"He has a bad leg. I have to take him to neighbor Stuart to pull that muscle on his leg. He sprained a muscle playing football." She praised herself for her quick thinking of finding that answer.

"Where is Stuart living? I have a bad leg

too."

She knew he has a permanent sore foot but made no mention of it. She wanted him to leave.

"Neighbor Zoffi, I'm going to finish cooking my pot."

"What about the dirty clothes in the tub?"

"I will do that later. I don't like my husband to come home and don't get dinner in time."

He left, and she couldn't wait to speak to Paul.

"Paul, did you hear the conversation between Thakur and me?"

"Yes, Mother."

"Do you know the Bible says you must not covet your neighbor's wife?"

"Mother, why are you telling me that?"

"Because Thakur is sharpening his machete for a nigger man, and it could be you."

"Why me?"

"Are you secretly having an affair with his wife?"

He did not answer.

"Do you know the woman who came disguised at the apprentices' graduation?"

He did not answer.

"Why aren't you answering my questions, Paul?"

He looked at her with a blank face.

"I have a sister in Clifton Hill, Port of Spain. We have not seen each other since we left Tobago over twenty five years, and I am going to write her right now to see if she will take you to live with her until you get that job at Trinidad &Tobago Electricity Commission. Here is the key to the drawer where I hid the money you gave me for your five years when you were an apprentice."

"Do I have to take the money now? Can I wait until you get a letter from Aunt Nellie saying that I can come and live with her?"

"In the meantime stay away from Rena."

Joseph came home early. "Paul, what are you doing home?"

"I just felt like taking it easy."

"The General Manager of TLL told you to come back and teach new apprentices in the workshop. Why don't you take up his offer?"

"I'm waiting for an offer from Aunt Nellie."

"Your lazy Aunt Nellie in Port of Spain who sits her ass down and lets her stupid husband do everything?"

"She's a teacher; she just doesn't do house work."

"What kind of offer she has for you?"

"Ask Madam Joe."

The table was set for dinner, and Madam Joe called on Alex to say the *Grace before Meal.*"

"Me, Mother?" he asked.

"Yes, you."

"Dear God, I thank you for this meal which is not corned beef in a tin that Fyzabad's lazy women prepare after they lose their money from playing that numbers game called *whe-whe.* My loving Mother is a diplomat. She is trying her best to prevent neighbor Thakur from cutting off my brother's neck with his machete. I know for sure the woman who came disguised to my brother's graduation is not Thakur's wife. She is Thakur's wife's twin sister. And dear God, don't let anyone ask me how I know that. Amen."

Everyone at the dinner table looked at Alex as they dished food into their individual plates. Because Alex asked God to grant him the favor not to be questioned, the conversation was on a subject that was never discussed around the dinner table before.

Madam Joe opened the discussion. "What is the best way to know if a woman is in love with a man?"

"May I answer?" Joseph said.

"I want Paul to answer first because I have been trying to get him to answer me on whether he sees Rena secretly, and he never answered me. I was always suspicious whenever Rena comes to keep my company when I'm washing downstairs. She had an ax to grind." Madam Joe smiled.

Alex shouted. "The ax she had to kill you, was it as sharp as Thakur's coolie gun?"

The dinner table had scattered food all over the table from the wind that came from their mouths full of laughter.

"Alex, an ax to grind means someone has a selfish object in view," Paul said.

"So Thakur has a machete grinding every night, and she has an ax in daytime."

The diners cracked up with more laughter. When everyone stopped laughing, Madam Joe asked, "Paul, what is the best way to know if a woman is in love with you?"

"A Creole woman or an Indian woman?"

"Any woman?"

"Let me give you the answer I heard from atheist John Jules. I wouldn't love a woman as how Joseph loves Mary, his wife, when he heard she was having a child named Jesus for another man."

"Paul, I told you to stop going by that atheist," Joseph said. "Do you prefer an Indian woman or a Creole woman to be your wife?"

"From my observation, a dollar in a Creole woman's hand lasts six days; but a dollar in an Indian woman's hand lasts one month."

Alex shouted: "In buying shoes, in buying less corned beef in a tin, or in buying Tobago bloomers? Madam Joe had told us whenever she got new bloomers in Tobago, she used to fall and pretend she fainted in school and opened her legs to let the children see her new merchandise."

Madam Joe confirmed what Alex said.

Joseph said, "Madam Joe, no more jokes. It is time for me to help you wash the dishes with one of your old merchandise."

Paul said, "The prize for the best sit-down comedian goes to Joseph the hater of atheist John Jules."

"Madam Joe, why are you pushing Paul out of your house?" Joseph said.

"Because he would not tell me if he's coveting his neighbor's wife."

"And what if he does?"

"Joseph, would you like atheist John Jules coveting your wife?"

"Coveting doesn't mean he is actually having the goodies."

"Ask Paul if he's having the goodies from his neighbor's wife."

"I will not. And you have no right to ask him that question."

"When his neck is on a plate, I hope you will not mind washing the blood away."

"The next time Ziffo Thakur comes to help you dip water to put in your tub, ask him which nigger's head is ready-made for his machete."

# 8

The sound of Thakur's blade on the grinding stone was the music of the night.

Two months had passed, and the bell rang on the rusty gate. Madam Joe was washing and thinking. She was exhausted in her thoughts as to whom Thakur will kill with his machete. Her only therapy was to see Paul, whom she loves with every fiber of her body, get on a train at Siparia and go to Port of Spain. She wanted him far away from Fyzabad. The gossips of Paul and Rena meeting in Lovers' Lane when Thakur was out of town were plenty. Whenever she asked Paul if he and Rena were romantically involved, he never answered her. She brought home "nice girls" to be in his company, and he'd go in his bedroom, lock the door, and look up the hill.

"Joseph, you are no help. You don't talk to Paul, and tell him that he should not mess with Thakur's wife. All your answers are: Thakur has a sore foot. Since Thakur married Rena under bamboo he cannot breed her, and he is less than a man. You are a man without empathy for your fellowmen. All you Fyzabad men who do not tell your sons to stay away from other men's wives are godless men. You all don't read the Bible that says do not covet your neighbor's wife."

The sound of the bell that morning got her nervous. She did not want to hear Thakur's voice or to see him knowing that his sermon while she washed would be "Madam Joe, I have a man to kill." She felt he came there to torture her so that she would confess that her husband or one of her sons is in love with his wife; and that son or husband's blood will be on his blade. He had told Boolitan, "So help me God! I will kill that nigger who is in love with my wife." Once he told Madam Joe he had counted the foot tracks from his house to hers. He said he had plaited the grass that led to his house one night; it was loose in the morning; he was sure it was a man from her house with a certain foot size that loose the grass while walking on it; and that foot size stopped at his back step. He also said he had washed all the drinking glasses in his kitchen, dried them, arranged them in a certain order, and when he came back home from the wedding in Marabella, he found the glasses not arranged in the way he left them, and a man's finger print was on a glass. Whenever he came to chat with Madam Joe, he made sure he did not use the Indian code word, Nigger, as when he and Boolitan are chatting in Hindi, but he used the civil word, Creole.

It was Steve Crooks who pushed the gate. "Madam Joe, I was at the post office; I asked if there is mail for you; and Miss Jacob, the post mistress, gave me this letter."

Steve's voice was a like a gift from the Almighty to her that morning. "Thank you, Steve. I'm praying for you, Tony, and Reynold. Are you all still robbing Sonnyboy of his marbles?"

"No, Madam Joe. We and Sonnyboy are good pals. We go by his Father, neighbor Boolitan, and pitch marbles in his yard. And neighbor Boolitan gives us cold lime squash after we are finished pitching."

"You all are no longer afraid of Boolitan's coolie gun?" She laughed joyously, rushed inside, and read the letter to Paul: *My dear sister, Little Lo, it was so nice hearing from you after all these years. It would be a gift to me if Paul comes and lives with me. Bassam is not too strong these days, and Paul will be a good help around the house....* "Paul, will you go? Please, go. I don't want Thakur to kill you. I hear you go down Lovers' Lane and meet Rena. Alex went to see an Indian man hanging in Avocat from a rope after he killed his wife who was in love with a Creole man. If that Indian man had got hold of his wife's lover, he would have surely killed him before he hanged himself." She looked at Paul. "I will write Nellie tonight, and I will tell her that you will come. Paul, will you go?" Tears fell on her wet clothes.

"Yes, Mother; but give me time to remain and teach the apprentices in TLL one more month."

"When you leave Fyzabad, coolie Thakur will have to look for another nigger's blood to be on his machete blade."

She wanted to ask him if he and Rena "are

still bouncing heads together." That was the term Fyzabadians use for "having sex."

Alex threw his book bag on the table and shouted, "Madam Joe, when are you putting out your first born for me to get his bedroom?"

"My first born would greet me and say, 'Good afternoon, Mother, how was your day?'"

"Good afternoon, Mother. How was your day? When am I going to get that room?"

"Soon, Alex, my impertinent son. Aunt Nellie wrote and told me that Paul can come and stay with her in Port of Spain. As soon as she writes and lets me know exactly when Paul should come, you, Joseph, and I will take Paul to Siparia to catch his train to Port of Spain."

"I can't wait for that day to come."

"Alex, last night I was thinking of something you said."

"What?"

"You said the woman who came disguised in her Indian garb at the apprentices' graduation is Rena's twin sister, Ria, not Rena. How do you know?"

"Mother, you sent me to learn Hindi from Padma Kumari. I can speak and understand

Hindi. But I never let Indian people know that I understand them when they are speaking in Hindi. I was in Delhi Road by Roy and Windell. Their niece, Dolly, is Kristen's friend. She told Kristen that Roy and Windell drove Ria to the apprentices' graduation."

"That Indian girl who sits on your lap in the bus told you?"

"Mother, she has a name."

"So Kristen told you?"

"Yes, Mother."

# 9

Paul was packed for his trip to Port of Spain to leave early in the morning. He did not want anyone to accompany him to catch the train. Nor did he want anyone to make a ceremony about his leaving. He hugged his parents, and his Mother gave him the money she had saved for him. She asked him to count it, but he didn't. He called Alex into his bedroom and asked him to teach him how to say in Hindi: GOOD MORNING. HOW ARE YOU? MAY I HELP YOU WITH YOUR GRIP? I LOVE YOU. Alex wrote the sound of each Hindi word in English syllables, and he made Paul practice to say them. Then he said, "Paul, are you going to help someone who will be carrying a heavy grip to the train?"

"Alex, I don't know what I will be doing tomorrow, but tonight I want you to ignore the sound of Thakur's machete on the grinding stone and go to sleep to get up early tomorrow to catch the TGR bus."

"When you leave Fyzabad, you think Thakur will still be sharpening his machete on the grinding stone?"

"I don't know, and I don't care."

"I think he is grinding his machete to kill you because he suspects you and Rena are in love. He got the poems you wrote for Ria hidden in Rena's grip. Rena had gone by Ria; Rena loved the poems; and she took the poems home. Rena had told Zoffi, swearing to the Indian God next to lit candles in his house, that those poems belong to Ria. He had told her, 'How could they belong to Ria, and they are hidden in your grip?' And whenever I go in the market, Doris drops word for me saying 'a nigger is screwing my wife.'"

"How do you know that?"

"Kristen told me."

"Alex, the only thing on my mind is to leave this gossipy place and get a job at the Trinidad & Tobago Electricity Commission in Port of Spain as a welder, and after some years on the job, I want to be a welding instructor to teach apprentices and share my knowledge with young people. Goodnight, Alex."

Alex woke up early and peeped into Paul's room. Paul's grip was already packed with his clothes, but Paul was not in his room. Alex was somewhat confused and wanted to ask his Mother if she knew where Paul is, but time did not permit. He picked up his book bag and lunch in a brown bag and raced to get his bus.

It was Thursday. Madam Joe had only washed Paul's clothes on Wednesday. She picked up Joseph and Alex's clothes, put them in a hamper, logged them downstairs, threw them in the tub, got the dipper, bailed out water from the drums with rain water, and began to wash. She washed Alex's clothes first because they were less dirty. She put them on the grass to bleach, and as she walked slowly to the tub to wash Joseph's oily blue docks, the bell on the gate rang, and Thakur spoke aloud.

"Madam Joe! Madam Joe! I've got to tell you what's on my mind right now: A nigger man's blood will be on my poonyah today. I could not sleep last night. Paul's blood will be on my poonyah today!" He said something else in Hindi. The only sound Madam Joe remembered was "Ram. Ram."

"Neighbor Thakur, come drink some water to cool your temper." She rushed upstairs and filled a tumbler with water from the goblet. She handed him the water, and after he drank it, she sat on the bench so close to him, that he pulled his leg away from hers.

"Madam Joe, I'm just back from the market, and I heard Fyzabad people, especially that stinking nigger-woman Doris saying your son, Paul, is Rena's man."

"Neighbor, that couldn't be. Paul is on the train going to Port of Spain to pick up a job with Trinidad & Tobago Electricity Commission."

"And my wife is not even home. She probably gone with him."

"Neighbor Thakur, do you know that creole woman, Debra?"

"Sure."

"You know she married Indian Jake who lives in Emmanuel Trace."

"Jake really married nigger her?"

"She was Jake's choice; and Jake was her choice. They sleep in bed together. They pooled their money together. They no longer live in the mud house. They have a nice board house. And Debra is having a child for Jake. Zoffi, was it a bad choice for them, a nigger and a collie, to get married?"

"I don't know."

"Do you still want to have my son's blood on your blade even though you have never seen him with your wife?"

"People told me they saw them together down NMC late one night."

"What if they saw Ria instead?"

"What if they saw my wife, Rena?" Madam Joe saw his temper was rising.

"Those Fyzabad gossipers could be wrong."

"They could be right! Right! Right!"

"Would you be happy if they are right so that you can kill my son?"

He did not answer.

"Would you be happy if they are wrong so that you can spend your hate time making love to your beautiful wife?"

"I'm always making love to my wife. I broke her in from a little girl. Her father gave her to me when she was thirteen, and I married her under bamboo in my Hindu custom."

"Did you ask Rena if she ever made love to a Creole boy before she got married to you under bamboo?"

He did not answer.

"You can ask me if I ever made love to an Indian boy before I got married to Joseph."

He did not ask her that question.

"Could you promise me that you will stop sharpening your poonyah so that I can fall asleep at nights?"

"Madam Joe, I cannot promise you that. It could be Paul that is with my wife. And, believe me, if I ever see Paul today I will cut off his neck with my poonyah." He took out his machete from the case, kissed it, and swore in Hindi.

He did not take the long road to go to his house by walking in front of Elaine Trotman and Lystra George's houses. He took the shortcut from Madam Joe's kitchen garden and walked up the mud track to his house.

Paul came hurrying home on the long road in front of the alligator dam by Lyris George and Elaine Trotman's houses to pick up his grip to leave for Siparia to catch the train to Port of Spain. A culture of Fyzabad was a child leaving home to live elsewhere had to say goodbye to nearly all the neighbors in the district. He kissed neighbors Lyris and Elaine last, and rushed inside his house for his grip.

"Mother! Mother! Mother! why are you trembling with such fear?" Paul asked. "What's wrong, Mother? What's wrong?"

"Paul, I'm so glad Ziffo Thakur took the shortcut through his vegetable garden to his house."

"Why? Why? Why, mother?

"Only God knows why."

He kissed her. "I love you, Mother."

"Run fast for a taxi to take you to the train in Siparia. God bless you, my first born."

"Thanks for the money you saved for me, Mother."

"Thank God for saving your life today, Paul."

"And I thank God for your wisdom, Mother."

"Run! Run! Run! Don't come back to Fyzabad. Don't ever come back to Gower's Well Road. I don't want Zoffi Thakur to cut off your head with his machete."

She knelt, and prayed aloud to God. Her tears were plentiful.

# 10

"Mother, only a day has passed, and I miss my brother so much."

"Alex, his bedroom is yours. Why haven't you moved in?"

"I will never move into his bedroom."

"Why, Alex?"

"I will feel like a traitor."

"A traitor?" Joseph asked, and he took over the conversation from his wife.

"Yes, a traitor."

"You made a pledge to him that you will never break?"

"I love my brother. I believe in him. For his five years of apprenticeship, he gave me pocket change from his pocket change. He always asked me about Kristen, and he always told me to respect her as a human being. And I should marry her. Whenever I get on the bus, Kristen keeps a seat for me and the first words that come out of her mouth are, 'How is Paul?' She told me once Paul invited her to have a soda pop with him at Metro's. She did all the talking, and he did all the laughing. Once I told Paul, in jest, 'I heard you had a soda pop with my coolie girlfriend.' He told me, angrily, 'She has a name. And how dare you call her a coolie.' I never called her by that ugly name again even when we are making jokes with each other. What is so great about my brother is his humanity. I will never sleep in his room. His bed will always be empty waiting for his long legs, and for his annoying snores.

"Father, I remember how you almost took out Paul's eyes. You and Mr. Mason, Lloyd's father, were chasing a fowl to kill for Sunday's dinner. You threw a stick with force after the fowl, and the stick hit Paul by the side of his left eye. The mark is still there. When we were small I used to tease Paul and tell him if he had lost his left eye, I would have been able to sit on the left side of his plate and take the meat on the left side of his face.  And his answer was, 'I would buy a glass eye and put it in because you are too dumb to know the difference.'"

His Mother and Father laughed heartily.

"Alex," Madam Joe said, "Thakur came to kill Paul today.  God is looking over Paul."

"How do you know, Mother?"

"Thakur took the shortcut and walked through my garden to go to his house.  Paul came home walking in front of neighbors Lyris and Elaine's houses."

"Kristen told me she knows Zoffi and Rena.  Both of them are friendly with her parents, and Zoffi always uses the word Nigger to describe Creole people.  Rena always tells him to say Creole people, and his outburst becomes wild whenever she corrects him:  You are a nigger lover.  Nigger people are stink like ram goats. They don't bathe.  They are lazy.  All they love is carnival to take off their stinking clothes in the street.  I don't know why the police don't hold them for their indecent behavior."

Madam Joe said, "Is that true?"

"Kristen told me all Rena told him was,

'Zoffi, are you still grieving for nigger Doris' bed because she left you for another coolie man?' He never said a word after Rena's question. I told Kristen Paul has gone to Port of Spain, and she told me Ria has gone to Port of Spain to work at J.T. Johnson."

"When?" Madam Joe asked.

"I didn't ask her when?"

"Why didn't you ask her? I never thought you are so attached to your brother," she smiled, "my first born. Did he ever tell you that I brought Jean Murray home to meet him, and he locked himself in his room and never came out? When she left he told me he hated her because she calls Indian people coolies. Had he told me that I would have forewarned Jean and tell her to apologize for her Mother's behavior. She got that behavior from her Mother. Alex, this distrust between the Indians and Creoles is so deep, and I don't think the ill feeling between us will end in my life time. Whenever there is voting time the nigger-coolie playbook is the politicians' Manifesto, and we vote race."

"If my brother happens to meet Ria in Port of Spain and they hook up, what would you do,

Mother?"

"What do you mean by hook up?"

"Become man and wife."

"Without my consent?"

"Why does he have to get your consent?"

"Boy, let us end this conversation right now."

"Why?"

"I have to cook dinner."

"Mother, answer this last question before you cook: What if I graduate as a solicitor, get a job in Mr. Misir's office in San Fernando; Kristen graduates as a nurse, gets a job in San Fernando General Hospital, and we hook up. What would you say?"

"You are not my first born."

Joseph watched his wife as she walked away from the dining table. He couldn't read whether she was annoyed or disappointed with Alex's sense of loyalty to another race. She could see Alex was not disloyal but human in his thinking. Joseph felt his wife's ethnocentrism, not judging another race with the same good thought as her race, went deep, even when she pretended the Indians and the Creoles are God's people. Her prayer, "We are one blood in the eyes of Christ" was like a whited sepulcher to atheist John Jules. Jules preached in the market on Saturdays when the crowds are shopping: "You Christians of Fyzabad will get the worst seats in God's big theatre wherever he keeps his first-come-first-serve concerts. All the atheists with my thinking will be in the orchestra seats."

While Paul was on the train bound for Port of Spain, Madam Joe picked up pen and paper and wrote her sister: *Nellie, those young Indian girls in Fyzabad are becoming creolized. They are not listening to their parents who are advising them to marry in their race. They are dating Creole boys. They are singing calypsos behind their parents' backs. They are playing in steel bands behind their parents' back. They don't want to marry under bamboo again. They are very pretty girls. But they are....*

She tore up that letter, and began writing another because in those days a letter stays about two weeks to move from Fyzabad to Port of Spain: *Nellie, how are you? I wish I had a telephone to speak to you like those Creole big shots living in Apex bungalows. Those Creole big shots think they are better than we, and they think they are white. Their behavior stinks. I hope this letter reaches you in good health. Tell Paul I love him, and he should dress properly for his interview at the Trinidad & Tobago Electricity Commission. He is very private like his Father and does not discuss his life with anybody, but you must try and get him to talk. I suspect he likes an Indian woman, and that Indian woman's husband wants to cut off his neck with his machete. So keep your eyes on him and turn away any Indian woman who comes to look for him. Yours truly, your loving sister, Little Lo.*

She addressed the letter, sealed it, and called Alex to run to the post office and mail it.

"Mother, can I mail it on my way to school tomorrow?"

"No. Go right now!"

"Did you tell your first born in your letter to Aunt Nellie that his room will remain empty? I will never sleep on his bed or dust his bed because I want him to drown in dust when he comes back to sleep on it."

"His Mother will dust his bed and will sleep on it sometimes."

"Kristen will dust our bed when we are married."

"Once upon a time, your Mother was your idol. Now that...."

"Mother dear, save your adjectives for my future wife. We are still school kids. We are not yet married. I'm going to the post office, and I will return before the spit in your angry mouth dries."

A month had passed and nothing about Paul was known. The sound of Thakur's blade on the grinding stone was still her alarm clock. She got up and cooked for Joseph and Alex. Joseph hardly spoke to her because he knew she was grieving to hear Paul and his banjo playing *The White Cliffs of Dover*. She and Paul chatted with each other, and she had told him about her girly life in Tobago. And whenever he teased her and told her how she stole Papa Lee's eggs, she replied, "God gave me the wisdom to be in charge of those eggs." Their laughter was loud as Apex Company's siren that told oilfield workers it was time to clock in. But their laughter never got him to divulge his private life.

Madam Joe found a way once to get Alex to

join in the conversation with Paul. She brought up the incident of when the Indian boy had told 8-year-old Alex, "Nigger, don't come back to my church; I will beat you up." She asked Paul, "If that Indian boy had told you that, what would you have done?" Paul's replied shocked her.

"Mother, there are more than five ways to kill a cat."

Give me five ways, Paul."

"I will give you two. I'll keep the other three for myself."

"Why won't you tell me the other three?"

"Because you may use them on me some-day."

"Why do you say that?"

"You are a nice Mother, but you have a re-proachful tongue."

"I'm praying for you, Paul, that one day you will have children who will judge you as you judge me today."

"Mother, I'm not judging you. I'm telling you the truth."

# 11

Paul boarded the train at Siparia which is the last terminus in south Trinidad. The conductor punched his ticket and said, "Did you see that beautiful Indian girl in car 5 behind you? I am one Creole man who will forget my race and hide her in my bosom if I were not an old man. Why not go and sit with her? I can give you a joke to tell her to make her smile."

"I have too much on my mind right now, sir."

"Like what?"

"My Mother is praying for me to get a job at T&TEC in Port of Spain, and having an Indian wife would be the last thing in my Mother's imagination. She knows an Indian man wants to cut off my neck with his machete because he thinks I'm his wife's lover."

"Are you?"

"No such thing."

"Then how that coolie man came to that conclusion?"

"I'm in love with his wife's twin sister. They are identical twins, and people tell him that they see me with his wife in Lovers' Lane."

"My first cousin is a big shot at T&TEC. This is his phone number. Call him and tell him Cacki says to put in a word for you. Don't disappoint me by any bad behavior if you get a job at T&TEC. What is your trade?"

"Sir."

"You forget my name already."

"Is Cacki really your name?"

"Practice calling me Cacki."

"Cacki, I am a welder. I graduated from Trinidad Leasehold Limited's workshop with first class testimonials. The General Manager begged me to remain and train the new apprentices."

"Do you know Ahmad Charles who works

in TLL?"

"I know of his fame as a great cyclist, but I don't know him."

"I beat him in a race at Siparia Fete."

"True?"

"If you happen to meet him, ask him the name of the man who beat him in the Siparia meet. When the train stops at Couva, I will come in after you and tell that beautiful Indian girl to move her grip from the seat to let you sit."

"And I will speak to her in Hindi."

"You can speak their language?"

"No. But my little brother who speaks Hindi taught me couple words."

"Don't forget our plan before a handsome Indian boy sits next to her. Go to sleep but get off the third stop from this one. The engineer will blow very loud when he is approaching Couva. Is that a deal?"

"A done deal, Cacki."

Paul went to sleep immediately. In his sleep, he dreamt of Fyzabad, the only place he knows. His mind roamed on Lovers' Lane where he and Ria met in the dark and spoke for hours. Their chit chats were about if they become more than friends would they become a family. Neither answered that question with certainty. But Ria showed more signs that their friendship could blossom into a joyous ending.

Whenever Paul was about to talk of his Mother and her anti-East Indian behavior, Ria would cut him off with two words: "Not now. Paul, I want you to know my sister borrowed the poems you wrote to me; Ziffo found them; and he thought you wrote it to Rena."

"How Thakur came to that conclusion?"

"He caught you peeping at Rena's bedroom at nights."

"That's not true. My bedroom faces Rena's, and sometimes when I'm closing my bedroom window my eyes naturally see her."

"Do you peep at her?"

"Ria, from the day I met you when I was riding to work, I never stopped thinking of you. I would never peep at a girl, only if that girl is you."

She laughed; Paul jumped on his bicycle and whistled *The White Cliffs of Dover*. They met at that very spot where they chatted every morning. He went to work, and she hurried off to catch the bus to go to Oxford Commercial College in San Fernando.

The engineer blew the whistle; Paul woke up, stood, stretched, and yawned. He picked up his grip and dismounted from the train. He did not have to look for Cacki. Cacki was walking close to his heels. People were rushing into the train, and Cacki went straight to the pretty Indian girl and said, "Miss, could you move your grip for this gentleman?" Before she answered, the gentleman whistled, *The White Cliffs of Dover*. She shouted, "Paul, Paul! That's you? Where are you going?"

Paul winked at Cacki who hurried to car 6. "Ria, where are you going?"

"I'm going to work at J.T. Johnson in Port of Spain."

"Coolie gal, you are going there to be a porter for white people. Only white people work in that store."

"Nigger man, come and hug me, and kiss me on my cheek. But not like nigger Judas."

Their laughter was contagious. Indian and Creole people were always politically correct in public places but to hear those two passengers say such things in public amazed them. Some of them put down their heads, pretending they were tying their shoe laces.

It was the first time that they hugged so passionately, and they never let go until the train rocked, negotiated the bend, and stopped at Chaguanas, in Central Trinidad. There Indian people were in the majority, and Creole people were called Negroes.

A little Indian boy said, "Mammie, why that Negro man is hugging that nice Indian lady so tight?" His mother answered, "Boy, come here and let me tie your shoe lacing. Next stop is ours."

"Why Mammie?" the child repeated his question.

Ria answered. "We are best of friends since we were children."

"Where do you and your Negro friend live?" The little boy looked at them.

"We live in Fyzabad. I have a lollipop. Ask your Mammie if you can take it."

His mother said yes. He ripped off the wrapping paper, put the lollipop in his mouth, and the crowd of Indian people and Negro people wished the little boy would have asked more questions. Not his Mother, because she knew her son would ask adult questions that would make her run quickly to the last car on the train.

Ria took Paul's hand from his side and put it around her shoulder. They looked into each other's eyes. They squeezed each other's fingers. Ria took out her hair from the net and asked Paul if he prefers it long or if she should cut it. He said, "If you cut one strand, I will drive my love picket into—you know where?"

"My heart. That is the only places your picket can go."

"Girl, you are getting fresh. Tell those north men that, and they will claim you heart after they put their pickets in. And you know where else they'll put their pickets?"

They hugged and laughed.

"Ria, never in my wildest dreams had I thought you will be going north on the same train, and on the same day with me."

"Alex told Kristen that you were moving out as soon as you get a letter from Aunt Nellie. You never told me but Kristen told me. I told my sister that I would accept the vacancy in Port of Spain. My Father was annoyed because I had told him that I would accept the bookkeeping appointment at Rahamut Stores in San Fernando which is nearer to Fyzabad. But when Kristen told me last month that you planned to go to Port of Spain to work with T&TEC I chose to work in Port of Spain hoping one day we will meet on the street. My Father always suspected that I had an ulterior motive. Fathers always think when their daughters change their minds they are moving away from them. I always re-read the poems you wrote for me whenever I'm lonely."

"Which one?"

"This one: People think so differently when they are sad from when they are happy/ The music from the fisherman's mouth calling for people to buy his fish/ Is so different from Madam Joe's singing *The White Cliffs of Dover* after she fries her fish/ We all make a musical sound when we pound our toe/ And I'm hoping for the day when I reach a climax to say ooh-ah/ With you.'"

"Did your sister get that one to read?"

"And Zoffi found it."

They looked at each other and smiled.

"Can I sleep on your shoulder till we meet Port of Spain?"

"When you reach, who will be picking you up?"

"I had been in touch with a friend who gave me the name and address of a woman who boards people who live out of town. You have some place where both of us can stay until we find a room where we can live as roommates?"

"I am going by Aunt Nellie who lives at Clifton Hill. The last time I had gone by her I was five years old, and all I remember of her was she used to pinch me and say, 'Boy, when I call you, you must come right away.' I told Aunt Nellie, I am my Mother's first born and my Mother waits until I come. Aunt Nellie replied, 'Little boy, you are not the first born in this house.'"

"Paul, I will pinch you very hard right now if you refuse to give me a deep kiss to let all the people looking at us know that we are buddies from Butler's Fyzabad."

"I will take as many pinches you have to give, and I will take you to Aunt Nellie and tell her this coolie gal was misbehaving in the train."

"And I will tell Aunt Nellie that this nigger

boy used to pee his bed. I know because Madam Joe told Rena." She spoke in Paul's ear. "We have an audience from the time you got in at Couva. Let us pretend we are fighting."

"Not with me." They laughed.

When they got off at the last stop at Marine Square, Port of Spain, there were Indian boys waiting to tote Paul and Ria's grips on their heads to their destination. Ria opened her purse, and Paul stopped her. He already had a shilling in hand when they reached Clifton Hill, also called East Dry River or Behind the Bridge, which was a low-income neighborhood.

Paul knocked once, and before his second knock, Aunt Nellie opened the door and screamed, "Little Lo's first born, I have been looking at my clock from the time your train left Siparia." She kissed, and hugged him.

"Aunt Nellie, this is my best friend from childhood, Ria Patel."

Ria stretched her hand.

"I don't want your hand, Ria. Let me kiss you, my child. If I knew you were coming I would have washed the red carpet for you to walk on."

"And I would have worn Cinderella's slippers?"

"You expect Prince Paul to marry you?"

"I hope one day he will propose."

"And don't lose my invitation."

"Aunt Nellie, Prince Paul had me cracking up on the train, and now you are doing the same."

"Now you have to eat. I am not waiting on my Tobago husband. He has to talk to every neighbor before he comes home; and if he comes home and says who is this pretty Baytee, don't feel bad."

"Aunt Nellie, I remember when Uncle Bassam used to say you are the prettiest girl who was born in Tobago," Paul said.

"You were a little boy. How do you remember that?"

"I have a good memory. Aunt Nellie, can Ria stay here tonight. Tomorrow she will be going to board by a friend."

"She can board here."

Ria shouted, "True!"

"Not if you pee your bed as someone I knew." She pointed at Paul.

"Aunt Nellie, I'm like a nurse. I walk with

many medications."

"Girl, you can stay as long as you like. You are my best looking niece."

"Aunt Nellie, can I help you in the kitchen or with any house chores?"

"This house has three bedrooms. The front bedroom is mine. You and Prince Paul can choose the bedroom you need—the one on top or the one downstairs. The one next to me is crowded with junk; the one downstairs is clean and uncluttered."

"Aunt Nellie, you know me first. So I should choose first."

While they were around the dinner table, Bassam walked in, and he tipped his hat as an elderly gentleman to Paul and Ria. He knew neither of them.

"Bassam, this is your nephew, Paul. He has grown tall as a palm tree. And this is Paul's best friend, Ria," Aunt Nellie said.

"Stay where you are. Don't move. Paul, you have really grown. You are no longer the little boy that Aunt Nellie pinched his ear. And young lady, you are a pretty Baytee." His wife looked at him. "Sorry. You are a pretty young lady."

"Thank you, Uncle Bassam."

"Bassam, wash your hands, and come and eat. A man came around selling red snappers, and I bought four. I know you like the head because you always say the head has phosphorous which is good for your manhood. And what is the tail good for, Ria?"

"Phosphorene."

"Aunt Nellie, why don't you ask me a question about the welding trade and why the longshoremen are about to strike on the wharf because the Indian welders get a bigger salary than they?"

Bassam said as he walked to the table, "I will tell you why. It is because those Calcutta coolies are working cheap for the wharf."

Paul was rife with anger as if he were the German lawyer, Hans Rolfe, who defended Ernst Yarning, the German judge who sent Jews to the gas chamber, at the Trial at Nuremberg. Paul shouted at Bassam for saying the words "Calcutta coolies." Paul knew Port of Spain Negroes had a grudge for Indians, and it became worse when the Indians became educated and held the major jobs in government, in business, in the constabulary, and they no longer toted the Negroes' load on their heads.

"Uncle, I don't like the term *Calcutta coolie*. The knowledge I have today was given to me by an Indian man named Mr. Oudit Mungal. After my apprenticeship at TLL, I returned to teach for a while and the Indian boys were ready and willing to learn and never hid in the bathroom. The Creole boys always had an excuse to stay home. Most of those longshoremen had the opportunity to learn the welding trade as the Indians but their minds were on quick money for their labor. In life some of us plant a pepper tree to get a quick crop; others plant an oak tree and wait until it grows."

"Paul, in Port of Spain we do not use the word Creole. In the north, we call ourselves Colored People, Negro People, or Black People. But many of us don't like to be called Black."

"Thank you, Uncle."

Aunt Nellie had her eyes fixed on Ria. Ria was aware of Nellie's direct stare on her. Ria asked Bassam to pour her more soursop juice. "Uncle Bassam, I will bet you all the money in my purse that this soursop fruit came from Tobago. And I will bet my first pay check that will be deposited in the Penny Bank that the soursop that made this drink came from Alma Road, Mason Hall."

"Ria, are you a botanist by trade? How do you know that?"

"Uncle, Ria reads many books," Paul said.

"Ria, I apologize for using the word coolie," Bassam said.

"Uncle Bassam, please don't. Paul and I called each other coolie and nigger on the train."

"In front of Black people and Indian people?"

"Paul and I were laughing at the expressions in their faces."

"Ria, from habit, I know I will say that word again, but never in front of you again. My spirit loves you, and I hope Lily allows you to stay as long as you wish."

"Why do you call Aunt Nellie Lily?"

"As a boy in Tobago, I couldn't steal Miss Ida's rose to give her on her tenth birthday because Miss Ida was in her hammock under her house. So I ran to the pond on Alma Road, I pulled out a water lily with all the roots, put it in a pan with water, hand it to her, and wished her happy birthday. Whenever you want to butter up my lovely wife to get a favor, call her Aunt Lily."

That was an evening of laughter.

# 12

Paul chose a white shirt for his interview at T&TEC. Ria changed it. "Wear a blue shirt. A working man looks better in blue. You are not going for a white-collar job."

"I like this yellow tie to blend with the blue shirt."

"Paul, you are not going to sing calypso."

"Then you choose my clothes and dress me."

She did.

She traveled with him to the employment office of T&TEC on Wrightson Road. Paul asked the receptionist for Mr. Johnson. The receptionist walked him to Mr. Johnson. "So you are Paul?

Where is the young lady that Cacki introduced you to?"

"Sir, she's sitting in the waiting room."

"Cacki said both of you are two peas in a pod. Go and get her before I change my mind."

Paul rushed outside, and he brought Ria in. She stretched her hand and held his grip. "I am Jan Johnson."

"I am Ria Patel."

"Are you in town to keep Paul's company?"

"No, sir. Tomorrow I will assume a position as a junior bookkeeper at J.T. Johnston Stores."

"Did you study bookkeeping?"

"Yes, sir. I got a first class testimonial in Advanced Bookkeeping from Oxford Commercial College in San Fernando."

"Do you still remember to do double-entry transactions?"

"Yes, sir."

"Balance sheets?"

"Down to the penny."

"You are very good." He turned his attention to Paul. "Young man, please, tell me something about yourself, and then tell me about your trade."

"Sir, I was born in Fyzabad, also called Grenadian town, and my Mother hates Grenadians."

"Why?"

"She's very provincial."

"Are you?"

"No, sir. My policy is let's live, and let others live…I am twenty two years old. My parents are Joseph Sears and Leoni Sears. Both were born in Tobago and migrated to Trinidad at age eighteen. They taught my brother, Alex, and me well.

"My Mother favors me more than my brother, Alex, who is three years my junior. She is an alien to cultural relativity. She does not judge another culture objectively. She calls Indian people coolies, not covertly, but in their faces. She uses her culture—and she calls it Creolism—as the standard by which to judge Indian people.

"My Father is so different. He believes in cultural relativity. He judges another culture objectively; and I am as he."

Mr. Johnson stopped him from speaking.

"Paul, Ria is also here to assist me in my interview of you." Ria looked at him in amazement. "Ria, is Paul speaking the truth?"

"Mr. Johnson, I don't know. He never tells me what takes place in his family. For that matter, we met on the train. I did not know he was coming to Port of Spain; and he did not know that I was coming to Port of Spain. We became friends when I was waiting for the bus to go to school, and he was riding his bicycle to TLL to learn trade. Whenever he was leaving after we chatted, he'd whistle *The White Cliffs of Dover*. He wrote me poems."

"Love poems?"

"Not really. His main theme of his poems was his imagination, a philosophy that was not akin to mine. My parents are Indians. I picked up the mangoes that fell from their trees; I looked at them; and I threw down those that I did not want to eat. That's my philosophy."

"You prefer apples to mangoes?"

"I prefer the fruit that I do not have to import."

He smiled. Before he asked another question, she spoke.

"Mr. Johnson, I hope my interview tomorrow at J.T. Johnston Ltd. is not as direct as yours. Nonetheless, your interview is good practice. I hope it is the precursor of good luck. I left home with both faith and fate in my grip with my clothes and shoes. I was offered a job as a junior bookkeeper in Rahamut Stores in San Fernando so if I did not get J.T Johnson's I will accept the post at Rahamut's."

"Ria, J.T. Johnson's has ninety nine percent Caucasians. We, the Blacks, call those French Creoles by our code names the NEs, Negroid Extracts. That term was coined by a Woodford Square anti-colonial politician. He said French Creoles hide their blackness, but the teats of their wives' breasts are black. He gave other anthropological examples which I do not care to lament on today. Most times the hats and shoes Black people bought did not fit them when they went home and tried them on.

"Ria, once upon a time Black people had to buy a hat or a shoe without trying them on inside the store. Your Fyzabad Butler's movement in 1937 in its Manifesto said to Black People in Port of Spain: DON'T SHOP WHERE YOU CAN'T WORK. And that manifestation from Butler changed J.T.J's policy somewhat.

"But I'm sure your fate would be that you'd

be employed. You are very smart. Look Maggie Magalange in her eyes when you are interviewed. She's like Queen Elizabeth. That means you can't change the subject when she's speaking. Come and look me up sometimes." He buzzed his secretary. She came in. "Miss Peters, take Miss Patel to the dining room, serve her whatever she likes, and keep her company. No calls. I'm going to interview Mr. Sears."

"Paul Sears, tell me about your trade."

Paul expounded for half an hour on his trade, and why he loves it. "Sir, I will like one day to be a welding instructor at this Commission. I love to share my knowledge."

"Before I retire, I will put in a word for you. Come in for your medical tomorrow. Do not dress up."

"Thank you, Sir. When you talk to Cacki or see him, tell him he is my angel."

––––––––––

Ria had never come to Port of Spain. She was offered a job as a junior bookkeeper in Rahamut Stores in San Fernando but she told her interviewer to give her a week to finalize a legal transaction with a solicitor over her grandfather's property. She had no such transaction to finalize. The only town she knows is San Fernando where she went to R.N.M. Donaldson Commercial College and graduated with first class honors in all her classes.

She left Aunt Nellie's house early because she did not know where she was going, and she did not want to walk fast and perspire. She walked slowly down the steep hill where she lived. She asked a school girl for direction to J.T. Johnson Stores. When she reached Charlotte Street she did not know whether she should cross west or south of the traffic light because the street merchants blocked the cars, and the cars ignored the red traffic lights. Luckily, the whole street was blocked and it gave her time to think. She walked west on Queen Street and turned south on Frederick Street. The streets were crowded with cars there too, and pedestrians did not obey traffic lights at the intersection either.

She looked at her wrist watch and saw she was three quarter of an hour early. She went into Ross's café at the corner of Frederick and

Queen Streets and bought tea. She did not need tea. She bought it to be able to sit in comfort. At Ross's café one could not sit without purchasing something. Ria did not know the customs of that café but she studied its customs when she stood outside and looked in. Fyzabadians are keen on reading situations, and they are conversant of the fact that city people call people from south Trinidad by uncharitable names; and it became a fact when she pretended she was enjoying her tea that she didn't care for. She already had her hearing antenna up because she knew that the two men sitting two tables away from her would be making her their breakfast topic.

"Harry, I'm sure that coolie 'oman is a county bookey in high heels?"

"She's a damn pretty Indian woman. How you know she's a country bookey, Frank?"

"By the way she's looking at everybody and everything."

"Probably she's a tourist."

"You want me to go and ask that country coolie where she came from?" He got up, and he stood still.

Ria's heart jumped. She became afraid

of what he may do to her. The only people she knew in Port of Spain were Paul, Aunt Nellie, old Bassam, and they were not there to let her know that those two idle men were just shooting the breeze. Had those trash talkers been in Fyzabad, she would have known them, their family background, whether they served time in jail, were they on the podium to receive commendation from Mr. Telemaque, the head master, whether they had gone to school with her and had been benched and flogged by the head master for cutting class, or whether their names were in Fyzabad's gossip dictionary.

Immediately she wondered why she didn't take the junior bookkeeper job at Rahamut Stores in San Fernando where the business is owned by a rich Indian family, people of her ilk, not in finance, but in race, people who would never label her a coolie. And her Father whom she loves would have been happy to see her home every evening.

She remembered Paul had written something and put it in her purse while she was dressing in the bathroom. She opened her purse, took out the white sheet of paper, looked at the two idle men, and read Paul's note softly: Look for the trash talkers at Ross Stores / Look for them before you cross the streets/ Look not at the traffic lights because they stick on red often/ Look for the haters at J.T. Johnson Stores/ Then look forward for your paycheck/ I need a loan to take you to a movie/ And get my first real kiss when the theater grows dark.

She smiled at the thought she'd be getting her first real kiss from Paul. Last night she thought he would have kissed her as his lover. All he said was,"Goodnight, Fyzabad's prettiest woman, and good luck at your interview tomorrow." She got up, pushed her chair in, and walked to the door.

"Have a nice day, country bookey," both men said.

She walked back to them. "Thank you, gentlemen. Are both of you fresh deportees from the cold Alaska?"

Shocked at her question, they stared her.

"It is fire hot outside, and I see you are wearing wool. Drop by J.T. Johnson's, and I'll buy you some cotton shirts. I'm a bookkeeper there, and I can more than afford to give you a dozen shirts each as an Easter gift."

A woman who was listening to the conversation ran outside with her coke and ham sandwich in her hand laughing and coughing.

Frank whom she thought was wearing brass knuckles and didn't know how to smile, said to Harry, "She's very beautiful, and comedic. I like her."

Her appointment was for 9.30 a.m. At 9.15, she looked in the mirror in the women's clothes department. She was satisfied with her looks, and she knocked the door marked Margaret Magalange.

"Come in."

"Good morning, Mrs. Magalange. I am Ria Patel."

"How are you, Ria? I expected you 9:30; and you are here exactly 9:30. Have a seat."

"Thank you."

"You traveled from Fyzabad this morning?"

"I came in last week."

"You have relatives here."

"No. I have good friends who live in Clifton Hill."

Mrs. Magalange displayed a strange look, and said, "Behind the Bridge?"

"I don't know what that means."

"Never mind. I have been looking over your qualifications for the junior bookkeeping job. Only last week that vacancy got filled."

"Does that mean you will not employ me today?"

"You will be employed. If that new girl does not work well with Mr. Stollmeyer, the head bookkeeper, and Coleen, his assistant, you will surely get that job."

"Would I be unemployed in the meantime?"

"Of course not. From tomorrow Hilda Hall will be training you on the floor in the men's department. You will get a fixed salary, but you will also get a commission on the sales you make. Ria, your bi-weekly salary plus your commissions will be more than that of a junior bookkeeper's. The person with the highest total sales each month will also get a percentage of her sale. What do you say about that?"

Mr. Johnson's advice came to mind, and she looked Mrs. Magalange into her eyes and said, "I thank you very much for this opportunity."

"Ria, if you were not getting a job, I would have asked you questions about your character first." Mrs. Magalange smiled. "I like your business look. I think you will fit in well here, sartorially. Is it the first time you've walked down Frederick Street?"

"Yes."

"Did you find your way without disturbance from idlers?"

"I had a little annoyance when I had tea at Ross's. I thought two men were giving me a hard time, but when I was leaving they told me, 'Have a nice day, Miss Beautiful.'"

"You are a beautiful woman, Ria. So nothing is wrong with that compliment. What else they told you?"

"One told the other that he is sure that I am a coolie country bookey."

"Were you offended being called a Coolie or a Country Bookey?"

"Neither of those terms offended me. I'm not a Coolie because I do not and never have I toted load on my head. My Father is a widower, and he employed someone to work for us. If I have to tote load on my head here, I will walk out J.T. Johnson in a nanosecond. Being called a Country Bookey by the two idle men in Ross Store shows not only their insularity but their dearth and paucity of the beautiful words in the English language to describe my rustic upbringing."

The phone rang. Mrs. Magalange did not pick it up. She was measuring in her mind what question she should ask Ria to confound Ria's flawless lyrical delivery. Ria's answers were so sociological in nature. "Ria, I always tell an interviewee to ask me two questions, but it is never a compulsory request. You are at liberty not to ask me any questions." She and Ria smiled simultaneously.

"Mrs. Magalange, on my way to your office, among other observations, I saw two colored women. I don't know if Black people prefer to be called Colored in Port of Spain."

"Ria, are you sure that is the question you want to ask me?"

"Yes."

"Ask me another question."

"Would you keep me in mind if an opening for a junior bookkeeper comes up?"

"I will, Ria. Tell me: Where do you practice your intellectual exercises?"

"To be current, won't you mind if I practice them here?"

"You already have like the wind that blows where it wishes. I will also keep you in mind for a managerial opening and for my living-room discussions with my husband. I'm looking forward to seeing you tomorrow. Welcome to J.T.J."

She stretched out her hand. Mrs. Magalange shook it, and smiled.

Ria couldn't wait to get home to tell Aunt Nellie she got a job. Aunt Nellie couldn't wait to tell her that she and Paul can stay downstairs as long as they wish because her niece from Tobago would not be coming to live with her as promised.

"What do you mean by you got a job? Does that mean you did not get the junior bookkeeper's job?" Aunt Nellie asked.

"I will be a store clerk in the men's department, and I will be getting commission."

"Are you disappointed?"

"I'm not. I will show my skill as a saleswoman. My Father is a butcher who sells in Fyzabad market, and all his customers are my friends' parents. All the customers who come to the men's department will come to me. I know how a country bookey can get city upstarts to buy from me. My commission will be bigger than all those white women's."

"Did they welcome you graciously?"

"Tomorrow I will see how the woman who will be training me will behave. I can't wait for Paul to come home."

"Ria, I want to talk to you before Paul comes home."

"Aunt Nellie, I was waiting for this discussion two weeks ago."

"Why?"

"Because Paul suspected his Mother will write you many letters about race relations among Indians and Black people."

"Of course, Leoni wrote me. She told me she is called Madam Joe in Fyzabad. How do you call her?"

"Paul never invited me to his house or to meet his Mother."

"Had you invited him to yours?"

"No; even though I live in Delhi Road, and Paul lives in Gower's Well Road which is near to each other. Ours was just a roadside friendship. On his graduation day from trade school, I disguised myself in a burka, and only my eyes were seen. I talked to no one, and I went and sat on a chair in the corner of the Senior Staff clubhouse. To see him graduate without letting him or anyone know was on my bucket list."

"In your apartment downstairs, you'll be living and sleeping in the same room, and I will not be watching you but I am of the old school. How old are you?"

"Twenty one."

"And Paul?"

"Twenty two; and Paul has never kissed me as a lover."

"Never?"

"Am talking about on my tongue. Never." She looked into Aunt Nellie's eyes.

"Now you make it difficult to say what I wanted to tell you, young woman."

"Paul put a note in my purse this morning. The note says that when I get my pay, he will borrow money from me to take me to a movie, and he will kiss me for the first time as his lover. When he comes tonight I will tell him that I'm waiting for that kiss."

"Bassam told me to invite you and Paul for dinner. And I told Bassam to think of what he's going to say before he speaks."

"Aunt Nellie, I like Uncle Bassam. Men his age are so used to say whatever comes to their mouths. My Father, too, sometimes, does not speak before he thinks; and he knows whenever he says something that I do not like him to say, especially when it concerns Black people.

"I have cold water in the fridge. May I bring a bottle of water when we come to dine with you and your loving husband?"

"Bring that man who is afraid to kiss you on the tongue."

They laughed aloud.

"Lily, who and you are laughing so loud in my house?" Bassam asked.

"My niece."

"Did you tell her I will be on my best behavior around the dinner table tonight?"

"We have not reached that part of your table manners as yet."

Paul opened the door. "Good afternoon,

Aunt Nelllie." He kissed her. "Good afternoon, Baytee." He kissed Ria on her cheek.

"Ria, what did he call you?"

"Baytee; that's an unmarried Indian girl."

"When both of you are arguing?"

"We never had an argument."

"In what world are both of you living? Don't keep us waiting, Paul."

"Aunt Nellie, me and me Baytee will be on time."

The dinner table had many dishes, and they were having fun as they ate. Bassam asked Paul about his job, and Paul was happy to speak of his job nonstop.

"Uncle Bassam, today I got wonderful news. I began working as an assistant instructor to the apprentices, and they wanted me to tell them the difference between arc welding and oxy-fuel welding."

"I did oxy-fuel welding when I worked at Neal and Massy, but at that time I knew nothing about arc welding. So I, too, will like to know the difference. Mind you, I do not want a long history about arc and oxy-fuel welding because my wife and my niece prefer to eat this delicious food when it is hot than to hear about what goes on at T&TEC nonstop."

"Oxy-fuel welding is a process that uses fuel gases and oxygen to weld and cut metals. Arc welding is a type of welding that uses a welding power supply to create an electric arc between an electrode and the base material to melt the metals at the welding point. Uncle Bassam, arc welding became commercially important in shipbuilding during World War II. I end my case, so let us eat."

Aunt Nellie said, "Paul, I heard you and Ria never had an argument. Is that true?"

"True as the Gospel of Paul Sears of Fyzabad."

"I also heard you are not romantic." Nellie laughed, and Ria put down her head.

"Uncle Bassam, do you want to hear about my apprentices?"

"Your love life is more interesting to us. Ria is a beautiful woman, and if you don't show interest in her, the young men who work on her job surely will. Port of Spain's men are not afraid of displaying their love in public. They don't wait for the darkness. The brighter the light the brighter their affection."

Paul looked at the trio. "Ria, I put a note in your pocket book this morning, what did I say?"

"It says when I get paid I must give you money, you will take me to a late-night movie, and you will kiss me in my mouth when the theater gets dark."

"Aunt Nellie, she gets paid bi-weekly, and she will be getting a lot of commission. So next week you will get my rent and my report about Baytee."

"What if she asks you to marry her under bamboo?"

"She is a Christian but if she does, my dowry will not be plenty."

"Paul, whatever is your dowry, my Father will find the money because I already told him that I'm in love with you. And since I was eight years old, I told him, 'Pa, I don't like your Hindu custom. If you force me to marry under bamboo, I will run away.'"

"But you have never told me that before."

"You left no opening for me to tell you many things. Whenever you felt I was getting possessive, you whistled *The White Cliffs of Dover* and changed the subject." She looked at Nellie and

Bassam, and said to them, "My sister's husband sharpens his machete every day to cut off Paul's neck. Paul pretends he does not know that; and whenever I tell him that my sister, Rena, told me that, he changes the subject."

"Why Rena's husband wants to cut off Paul's neck with his machete? What's his name?"

"Zoffi Thakur wants to kill Paul because people tell him that Paul and Rena hang out late at nights in National Mining Company road commonly called Lovers' Lane. Fyzabad's main culture is gossip; my sister and I are identical twins; and the gossipers took me for Rena, and made their report to Zoffi. The gossip about us is that Paul's Mother hates Indian women because she believes one day Zoffi will kill Paul. Zoffi goes by Madam Joe when she's washing downstairs of her house to chat with her, but his motive is to see if Paul will come home when he is there to kill him in front of her. He hates when Madam Joe boasts of Paul as 'My first born,' and since Zoffi is married he hasn't a child. He told my sister, and my sister told me that he said, 'I will kill your nigger and then you; so both of you could never meet in Lovers' Lane.'" She is born Hindu, but she's ecumenical from her early teaching.

Nellie asked, "Paul is that true?"

"If that is true, my Mother never informed me." He knew he was lying.

"Did your Father inform you of Zoffi's plan?"

"No. But my brother, Alex, did."

"Ria, why didn't you tell Paul his life was in danger with Zoffi?" Nellie asked.

She stayed a long time to answer. "Paul would not let me tell him. Many nights I went to bed and prayed that Paul and I will run away from Fyzabad and be happy in some distant land."

Bassam spoke. "Paul, Ria loves you. Can't you see?"

"Not even the pendulum of the clock can record my love faster for her."

"Paul, you are too young to behave as men in my time who never express their love to their women and wives. They wait for the darkness at nights in the bedroom to be sexual. I told you this before. Lily, you have anything to say to Paul."

Nellie said, "Paul, do you know what your

Mother said in her letters to me?"

"Yes."

"Her letters were sealed. How do you know?"

"She sent Alex to mail them; he opened them; and he told me what were in those letters."

"Did you tell Ria what were in those letters?"

"No."

"Would you object if I give Ria those letters to read?"

"Aunt Nellie, I love Ria more than anything in the world. I will never hide anything from her. Please, give them to her."

Aunt Nellie pulled the letters from her apron pocket, and she rested them on the table. Paul moved the letters, and he handed them to Ria. Ria put the letters back into Aunt Nellie's apron pocket.

Dinner was over. "Lily, it was a good dinner. I think I will go down by the pond and look for water lilies for you. Paul, every Friday when you are coming from work, I want you to bring a rose for my niece. You promise?"

"Uncle Bassam, I will keep that promise till I die."

# 13

J.T. Johnson Ltd. was a Trinidad's shopping paradise in its heyday. The front view of the large department store was on Frederick Street in Port of Spain, the capital of Trinidad. The Anglican and the Roman Catholic Cathedrals are less than a quarter mile from J.T. Johnson. When Ria reached the corner of Queen and Frederick Streets, she looked across the street at Ross's, and smiled as she remembered the two men who called her a coolie-country bookey. She looked at the huge clock west of Frederick Street, and knew she had fifteen minutes to stroll to work and be on time on her first working day.

"Good morning, Mrs. Magalange. How are you?"

"Very well, Ria. In a minute Coleen will be here to introduce you to the full staff, and then she will introduce you, personally, to Hilda Hall who will be training you. Do you need a notebook?"

"I walk with one."

"You don't trust your memory?"

"My notebook augments my memory."

Coleen walked in.

"Coleen meet Ria. Ria meet Coleen."

They shook hands, walked away from Mrs. Magalange, and chit-chatted to the lunch room that was empty.

"Coleen, I want to cut my hair to look as yours, but my boyfriend doesn't want me to cut it. Can I touch your hair?"

"Sure. How long you and your boyfriend are going together?"

"Since we were in school."

"For how many years now?"

"More than five."

"Are you thinking of getting engaged?"

Mrs. Magalange walked in. "Coleen, here are two rule books. Let her read hers now." She walked out of the room.

Coleen and Ria ended their conversation.

"Ria, this is the company's book of rules. Every new employee must read it."

"Coleen, can I ask questions after I've read it?"

"Of course. I will return in an hour to discuss the contents of the book. By the way, I was impressed with what I read in your resumé. In addition to your accounting knowledge, I read of your wide study in sociology, trade unionism, world affairs, and public relations."

Ria read and re-read the one hundred and twenty five pages of the rule book. She questioned herself if this is a company that she should work for. She got up, went to the water cooler, drank deep, and spoke to herself. "My Principal, Mr. Donaldson, had told us when he lectured us in bookkeeping classes that life in the corporate world is not what you may imagine when preparing a balance sheet for your exam. The balance sheet is an abstract document with figures. One day you may have an opportunity to read the rule book of a corporation. Then you'll ask yourself where do I fit in with the corporation's balance sheets that display black and red—gain

and loss—without the mention of social con-
tracts?"

Coleen walked in and disturbed her
thoughts. "Ria, are you ready to tell me what
you think of the rules that you have read?" She
opened her copy of the rule book in her hand.

"I like the company's medical; I like the
company's time off for a death in the family; I
like the company's commendation award for the
top salesman; and I think I will win that award
this month, or, for the latest, next month."

"For the past five years Elizabeth McBride
won that award."

"I know I can beat her."

"How?"

"You'll see."

"What would I see?"

"In what department you are placing me?"

"Rita Byden asked to be transferred from
the men's department to women's dresses, and
since an old employee has the first choice, I will
put you in her place. Is that agreeable?"

"The rule book says so, so it has to be so."

" Any questions about the rules?"

"On page 19, my interpretation of that

compound sentence is: I should address certain class of people differently from another class of people when they walk into the store? Is there a misplaced modifier in that sentence? Why should that be?"

"That is not my interpretation."

Mrs. Magalange walked in without knocking. "Coleen, you had sufficient time to go through the rule book. Take Ria on the floor to the men's department after lunch to meet Hilda Hall."

Ria was laughing in her mind like Brae Rabbit: "Don't throw me into the briar patch of the men's department." She took the lunch time to walk down Frederick Street to Marine Square and her memory was fresh. She saw a train moving into the depot the same time she and Paul landed on that tenth day of December. She had to call Paul.

"Hello."

"Paul, you know who is calling?"

"The coolie girl I love."

"How much you love me, nigger?"

"So much."

"I can't see how much."

"Coolie, I have both arms opened wide."

"Blackie, I am on my lunch time. Is Frederick Street far T&TEC?"

"Yes. I am on Wrightson Road, and it is a long distance from J.T. Johnson. Why do you want to know?"

"I want to have lunch with you. I'm quivering inside."

"Me, too."

"I can't wait for tonight. A nice man who is working in the Railway office allowed me to use his phone when I told him I came from Fyzabad, and I don't know the neighborhood. Guess who he is?"

"I can't guess who."

"Reynold James. He said Fyzabad has a rumor that you are hiding in the mountains because you are afraid Thakur will cut off your neck."

"How does Tobago Reynold look?"

"Great. He has a paunch. He told me Steve Crooks is a male nurse working in St. Ann's Hospital, and Tony George works with a private contractor. Is it possible that one of these days we can have our lunch together?"

"Sure."

"I'm walking back to work. I love you, Paul." She laughed. "I am going back to be trained by someone I will meet for the first time."

"I love you more, Ria. Get back to work for us to save money to buy a two-seat bicycle to ride around the savannah." He laughed aloud.

She smiled as she walked into the men's department.

"Ria, I am Hilda Hall."

"I am Ria Patel. Nice to meet you. How long have you been working in the men's department? "

"From the time I left school. My grandfather worked here all his life as a porter, and he pulled a string for me. So here I am—one of few colored people. Did you read the rule book?"

"Only this morning."

"Well, you will know how to speak to a certain class of people compared to another class of people?"

"What do you mean?"

"Ria, don't bull shit me! I don't think I will want to work with you. I didn't like the other bitch. She's a liar. And now you!"

"Hilda, I'm sorry. I read the racial slant in the rule book. I'm not a liar. Would you have time for us to go and sit on Marine Square benches and girl talk about the rules after work?"

"I'll take you to Woodford Square. You'll enjoy there. All the bush politicians and city slickers will be there lecturing about what they don't know. You may even find an honest lover coming from the Red House with an empty brief case, but he uses that briefcase to look important. Do you have a boyfriend?"

"Yes. He is the love of my life."

"Let me show you the shoe storage first. Tomorrow I will teach you everything about the suits."

"How come you never beat Elizabeth McBride and win that commendation medal?"

"I just never did."

"Would you doubt me if I say I would beat her next month?"

"Sister, I will drink to that. But after you beat her for the prize, look out for those French Creoles, those so-called-Trinidad-white people would be carrying news on you. Why are you laughing?"

"In Fyzabad, we call Negro people Creoles."

"In Port of Spain we call them by an underground name, the NE's (Negroid Extracts). When Magalange, that NE bitch, said I live behind the bridge in my interview, I did not take communion from my church that Sunday."

"I live behind the bridge too. Why you did not take communion?"

"I cursed that NE, and when I told my boys how she described me, they cut her tires three times that week. And when my grandfather who worked there for over thirty years told me she's having an affair with her Indian driver, I told myself the next time she tells me I'm a child from behind the bridge, I will tell her so too is that coolie man she's sleeping with. She treated me in that interview as if I live in a cave."

"Now both of us have to get that commendation award."

"Now that you understand everything about shoes, tomorrow we will go with the men's clothes."

A white male customer walked into the men's shoes department.

"Let me see how you can flirt with that NE as if you are in your night pajamas, Ria Patel."

"You'll see my skill as a gal from behind the bridge. I do not sleep in pajamas. I sleep in my panty only. I'll bet you he will purchase a pair of shoes."

"I do not bet. My Father plays the numbers game and never wins. I will not be a fool like he is."

"Where is the lady who works here?" the customer asked.

"I'm so sorry, sir, that she's no longer in this department for your purpose. May I help you, if you wish?"

"You don't speak as we northerners."

"You are correct. I know northerners call southern country folks by a different name."

He smiled.

"You don't like my country look, and that's why you smile?"

"Contrary to that."

"To what?" She smiled.

"Now why did you smile, Miss?"

"Is it a rule that you should not call my name?"

"You have not told me your name, so Miss

is my alternative."

"Alternative or your preference? Sir, my name is Ria." She smiled.

"Your smile is bothering me in a nice way. Could I have size 9 of this shoe?" He pointed.

She went to the stockroom and brought back sizes 9 and 9-1/2. He tried on size 9 and said, "Ria, how do you know the larger size would be my preference?"

"If you play golf, an alternative gives a better swing."

"You play golf?"

"No. But I've seen photos of you." He looked at her.

"Ria, I'll take the 9-1/2."

"I thank you for giving me my first sale, on my first day of work, sir."

"You haven't asked me for my name."

"Don't tell me. Let me guess when your family walks in with you tomorrow."

"I wanted to say you are beautiful and end there. But now I would say your beauty is a weapon, and I do not have a family."

Please, return."

"Ria, you know I will."

Hilda rushed to her. "He only buys from

Rita Bryden. How you got him to purchase shoes from you? He is very fussy."

"He had the choice of an *alternative or a preference*, Hilda." Ria looked at Hilda and put her left thumb up.

"I heard when you mentioned alternative as opposed to preference. Are they words golfers use on the golf course?"

"What the hell do I know about golf? I knew they are English words, and I applied them loosely to know if he's a wordsmith."

"I've begun to see your skill versus the company's rule book."

"I know you would."

"Ria, it's time to leave this place. I can't hang out with you this afternoon. Let's give it a rain check."

"Thanks for all your help, Hilda, and for not calling me a country fool."

"The day you hurt my feeling, and put these twisted Negroid Extracts in front of me, I will."

"That day will never come."

They laughed aloud as they stepped out of J.T. Johnson.

# 14

Ria changed her heels, put on sneakers, and ran home. As she opened the door, Paul handed her a bouquet of red roses. She threw the bouquet on the table and hugged him. And for the first time she kissed him as her lover. He repeated her deep kisses, and he kissed her as his lover.

Then they stripped.

"Paul, draw me closer to you. I love you more than life. You will be my touchstone until the day I die. I see the *White Cliffs of Dover* in my dreams every night from the first day you whistled that song for me. I hope we'll travel by boat to those Cliffs one day on our way to France. My love, I never thought this day will come. When I called you on the phone today, every part of my body was calling you."

Paul put his hand on her lips. "Ria, forgive me for stifling my love for you all these years. In Lovers' Lane when we sat close on the stump, and I felt the warmth of your legs, I prayed for the time when we'll be together as one without pretense as we did in Fyzabad. When I whistled *The White Cliffs of Dover* in the machine shop, the other apprentices asked me if that's the only song I know. I told them I'm whistling that song for my secret love. Now my secret love is here."

She kissed the lower part of his body, and he pulled her up. He kissed the lower part of her body, and she said, "No. Not now." She came on top of him, and he turned her over. "Ria, you are so beautiful. When we have our own home I will bring an artist to paint you naked. When you called me today, I was thinking about you. When I bought the roses I was thinking about you, and I rushed home to throw petals on the bed for you to lie on. For every day that I live I will breathe for life for your sake. Having you as my lover is the only gift I want for the rest of my life."

"Paul, this Baytee will dry your body when it is wet with my hair. I will stop each day to say a prayer for you. And I will remember tonight is the first night that I come home and roll on the petals of red roses. Tonight is my first taste of what heaven is. I love you."

They made endless love. They kissed as novices with renewed passion. Then he kissed her below, and she said, "Yes."

He looked into her eyes. "Are you sure?"

"I'm sure, Paul. Let it be. I will fall on my sword for you at this moment."

"My sword is sharper, and I will fall the same time with you."

Three hours later she put the long-stemmed roses in a vase. Paul had come home early, and he had cooked. They ate from each other's dish, and fed each other in their birthday suit.

"Honey, do your apprentices like the way you teach?"

"I think so. But there is one young man who told his friends that I sound like I live in deep country, the country bookey type."

"Who is he?"

"A Creole like me."

"In Port of Spain, nobody says Creole. Some say Colored, some refrain from saying Black. I'm confused at times."

"Thank you, Ria-come-lately city girl."

"How do you intend to handle that apprentice who is calling you a C.B?"

"One day I will sit in the class, and I will let him come to the blackboard and teach."

"What's your purpose for letting him teach the class?"

"When he's finished, I will commend him."

"Your commendation will make him stop calling you a country bookey? Or do you have a hidden motive?"

"I'll bet you it will. Tell me about your job after you read the rule book."

"I had my first sale. And I told Hilda this month I will get the commendation award for being the highest-selling salesman."

"Who was your first customer?"

"A Negroid Extract who made it his business to tell me he hasn't a family."

"Who is a Negroid Extract?"

"An NE is the underground word Black

people in Port of Spain use for French Creole who think they are white, English white."

"You are learning the city slangs faster than I. What dress did you wear?"

"I wore the dress I made on Aunt Nellie's hand machine."

"Is that the dress I ripped off from you tonight because it fitted all your curves?"

"That's the one."

"Let me know when next you are wearing that dress so I can come and have lunch with you."

"And let's suppose the man without a family, who plays golf, and is a member of Country Club, comes to give me a big sale, and he tells me that he wants to take me to lunch, what should I do?"

"Since in grade school, I never answer a hypothetical, Ria. But doesn't J.T's rule book say in a technical way: People who live behind the bridge should know their place?"

"I am Ria, not a population."

"I'm getting jealous, so please answer my question."

"Rena told me never marry a man who

gets jealous by just thinking that one day his wife will leave him for an imaginary man. You know who and what I'm talking about. Zoffi wants to kill you because he thinks you are in love with his wife since he read the poems you had written to me that he found in Rena's grip hiding under her clothes. And the fact that Fyzabad gossipers could not tell the difference between me and Rena, they took me for Rena when they saw you and me in Lovers' Lane. This man is a rich customer, and I want to bait him to buy shoes and suits to win that commendation award."

"By doing what?"

"By going to lunch with him."

"I will make it an easy choice. I will have lunch with my apprentices every day."

He went and washed the dishes. She made up the bed, and swept the rooms.

Aunt Nellie knocked.

"Come in."

"May I ask Bim and Bam who cooked today?"

"Paul cooked, Aunt Nellie," Ria said.

"I was smelling his curry from upstairs. What's on the meal, Paul?"

"Cavali fish, white rice, green pigeon peas, cabbage, avocado, aubergine, salad, green banana, okras, and salad."

"Your acidifying and alkalizing foods make me feel hungry; but, Paul, nobody can cook cabbage better than your Mother."

"How do you know that?"

"She is my older sister, and we lived in the same house in Tobago. And, by the way, your Mother wrote me and told me you never wrote her since you left Fyzabad. Why have you not written her?"

He did not answer.

She did not force him for an answer. "How is the job, Ria?"

"Aunt Nellie, I did my first sale today."

"Men's shoes or men's suits?"

"Shoes."

"A big foot or a small foot?"

"He asked for size 9, and I brought him 9 and 9-1/2."

"The Stollmeyer type of French Creole or the Hannays kind of uppity Negro?"

"Aunt Nellie, I'm from Fyzabad. I do not know these northern descriptions of Port of

Spain people. Is he English or Negroid Extract?"

"So you know the underground term Black people use. I was an elementary school teacher; I worked as a polling station advisor; and I was in a position to know those people and their attitudes. Now you have to add your country sociology to meet this city's. Let your beautiful looks lead you right. The Stollmeyer type will pick you up as his servant, let you jump in the back seat, and drive you to an unknown destination where you can be compromised. The Hannays type will show you off only for a time after you are compromised. Those two namesakes combine money and politics in Port of Spain, and they go hand in hand with their prejudices."

"Aunt Nellie, I don't know what you mean."

"Don't be fooled in this town. Don't let the shadow become the bone that you snap for."

"I'll remember that."

"Paul, the next time you cook, I will be supplying the water. Are you all comfortable down here?"

"Why do you ask?" Ria said.

"Do you hear your uncle's snores down here?"

"We are too busy doing our thing to hear him snoring."

Nellie laughed. "What a lovely bouquet?"

"Aunt Nellie, that came from the man I'm going to marry."

"When?"

"You'd be the first to know."

# 15

Every morning they kissed on the lips, and took their individual route to work.

And for the next two years they were very happy living in Port of Spain.

They went to football matches in the park and joined in arguments with strangers as to which team was better. They went to the oval to see the West Indies versus England in cricket matches, and the West Indies won the series. They went to see the world's three W's—Weekes, Worrell, and Walcott, great cricketers from Barbados with their individual batting styles. They went to see Sir Garfield Sobers who held the highest score in test cricket at that time. They went to see the finals between Malvern and Maple, arch rivals, and Malvern won. But they always love the same team. They won together; they lost together when they bet on three-card Monty. Guides took them to the Caroni Swamp to see flamingoes fly to their habitat in the setting sun. They went to see many American performers—Marian Anderson, Paul Robeson, The Globetrotters, Joe Louis, and their favorite performer was Johnny Nash who ended his concert with the song *For All We Know, we may never meet again.*

They went to jazz shows to hear performances by pianists Felix "Sugar Fingers" Roach, Ralph Davies, and guitarist Sunny Denner; they went to many calypso tents to hear the leading calypsonians, especially Sparrow, and Melody. And they finally found their way into Woodford Square, the mecca of knowledge and misinformation. It is the place where politicians come and speak, charlatans come and teach; churchgoers come and preach and their admirers sit on the grass and imbibe the lecturers' news of the day.

Paul and Ria took public transport to Carenage Beach and made love in the water and on the sand. Their behavior in north Trinidad was bold and carefree. In Fyzabad, their behavior was pretentious.

"Honey, after that lovely day on Carenage Beach and you taking your hair to dry me, I don't want to go to work this morning. Next time I'll ask Reynold to take us to Maracas Beach. Let us stay home today."

"Paul, I won the commendation award last month for the best salesman. I want to win it again this month to beat Elizabeth McBride's record. I promised Hilda we will hang out in Woodford Square this afternoon and girl talk. She told me there's a rumor circulating about me."

"By whom?"

"She'll tell me after work. Can you end your hugging and let me go and make breakfast?"

"You want to repeat what you did to me last night?"

"Would you let me go to lunch with the man who plays golf at Country Club to boost my sale?"

"Do you remember how Aunt Nellie described that type?"

"I will not be going in the back of his car like his servant girl. I will be taking a simple lunch at Ross's with him."

"What if those two idlers see the coolie country bookey from Fyzabad with the Negroid Extract?"

"I didn't think of that." They laughed aloud.

"Ria, since you are not going in the back seat of his car like his servant, that's fine with me. But don't wear the same dress you wore when you met him."

They laughed.

"My lovely coolie, can I get it now that I've given you permission to go with the Negroid Extract for tea?"

"Sure."

"What's his name?"

"James, shortened for Jim." But she did not tell Paul that she and Jim had met at Ross's before, and they had a snack at the same table many times.

Their lovemaking was passionate.

"Honey, call Jim's name and see if calling his name will turn me on." It did.

"Ria, now I'm afraid of what that man's

presence could have on you."

"Tonight I'll call Ruby's name and see if it will turn you on."

He laughed, and he imagined his laughter reached Gower's Well Road where he and Ruby met by the well and made love when nobody was there. But he never knew Ria knew about his friendship with Ruby.

For work that morning she wore a flair dress she sewed on Aunt Nellie's hand machine. The color of her dress was beige. Her shoe was black pomp. She weighed herself. "One thirty. I'm heavy. I have to drop five pounds to fit my five-nine height." She looked in the mirror and shouted, "Paul, come and hook me up, and see if you like this dress."

"Honey, I like it. Now I feel to do what Fyzabad's oilfield men do when their wives are beautifully dressed.

"What?"

"They make their wives take off their clothes after they are dressed and have sex before they leave the house."

"I am not your wife, and I don't live in Fyzabad. You forget?"

They laughed as they walked out of their apartment.

"Honey, what would you be teaching your apprentices today?"

"I will be teaching them the correct way to hold the welding torch the same way I hold my torch when I'm putting it in."

"I hope you'll be thinking of Ruby when you are putting in your torch tonight."

"How would you welcome your first male customer, if he is comes for a pair of shoes?"

"I will look at his crotch and say, 'Sir, I know what your size is.'"

"You are not the decent Fyzabad girl I once knew."

They laughed aloud and went their separate ways.

As she walked in, Hilda greeted her. "Ria, don't forget we have a date after work."

"Can't wait, girl."

Ria had a bonanza with sales, and she gave Hilda some of her commissions by putting Hilda's name on the sale slips.

"You, you, is this the black salesgirls' department?" a middle-aged woman asked.

Ria heard the question but did not look at the customer.

"I'm talking to you who pretend that you did not hear me. I'm going to report you to my sister."

Ria purposely went to a customer and said, "May I help you, sir."

"I'm trying to make up my mind. Which of these two suits will look better on me?"

"Sir, this gabardine will take you like Clark Gable; and this serge will fit you like Robert Taylor."

"My wife and I always have an argument about those two men."

"About what, sir?"

"Who is better looking? Have you seen any of them in movies?"

"I saw Clark Gable in *Gone With the Wind*; and I saw Robert Taylor in *Waterloo Bridge*."

"So you are a movie fanatic?" He looked at her from head to feet; and she could see that he was also studying her spice complexion.

"In my little town in Fyzabad that was all my fun."

"So whom do you think is better looking?"

"My twin sister, Rena, said if she had her way she would marry Clark Gable; and if I had my way, I would marry Robert Taylor."

"I have been coming to J.T.'s for over twenty five years, and it is the first time I've had such a lovely conversation. I wear size thirty eight. I will take both suits."

Mrs. Magalange called Ria. "I want to see you when you are finished with the customer. It's urgent."

The man heard. "Maggie, how are you? How is Dexter? At the Club, my children and I will be having a surprise party for Henny's seventy-seventh birthday. Did you receive my invitation?"

"Yes."

"This salesgirl is the best. I came here to buy one suit, but her knowledge of the movies made me buy two."

"She brought up the movie talk to you?"

"Of course, not. Seeing she was pleasant, and I didn't really care for help, I brought up the movies thinking she was ignorant and would walk away. But I was shocked. I'm bringing Henny next time to talk with her, and to ask her who is

better looking—Robert Taylor or Clark Gable?"
He turned to Ria, "What's your name?" Ria told
him. He turned to Mrs. Magalange. "Maggie,
Ria's a good product. She's my girl whenever I'm
at J.T.'s."

"Jack, tell Henny...."

He interrupted Maggie. "Here's one more
Ria: Who are the stars in *Casablanca*?"

"Bogart and Bergman."

"In *Hellscat of the Navy*?"

"Ronald Reagan and Nancy Davis who became Mrs. Nancy Reagan."

"I'll invite you to Country Club next week
to battle with the boys."

The other salesgirls, who waited with anx-
iety to hear Mrs. Magalange demand Ria to her
office because Ria ignored the woman who came
looking for the black department, walked to the
water cooler but they didn't drink.

Mrs. Magalange said, "Ria, don't bother to
come to my office."

"Come later, Mrs. Magalange."

"No. I don't need you again."

Hilda pinched Ria. "Lend me your white
angel sometimes for her to teach me how to use

J.T.'s rule book to my advantage to shit on those NE's faces."

"Time for us to leave, girl. Let's go and sit in The University of Woodford Square and bad-mouth the NEs." They were there in ten minutes.

"Ria, that NE bitch who came to mess with your head made another Black woman lose her job."

"The woman who lost her job, what she did?"

"She lost her temper, and she cussed that stinking NE. But your silent insolence embarrassed that bitch. NEs cannot take dumb insolence from Black people."

"What is this gossip going round about me?"

"I heard you and Jim meet regularly at Ross's. You have your mind on him?"

"I never planned to meet him at Ross's. We just met."

"More than once?"

"About three or four times."

"Why so often? Are you tracking him down?"

"No."

"Do you suspect he has his eye on you?"

"He gave me my first sale; and now he buys often from me. What I notice is that he comes and buys from me when you are at lunch."

"He is a great golfer; and he has admirers galore."

"Is that so? I'm thinking of going to see him on the greens."

"That is so. Have you told Paul about him?"

"No. There is no need to."

"What you and he spoke about?"

Ria took some time to think. "Oh…I told him in our conversations that he's so sure of himself…He told me he lives somewhere in Diego Martin…and he drives on weekends to Maracas Beach…I told him that I've never gone to Maracas Beach, and my boyfriend and I will hire our friend, Reynold James, to take us there…He said why not hire him because he only charges five cents a mile…I said that is too expensive… He said he will reduce the charge to one cent… Things like that we talked about."

"And you did not tell Paul about your three or four meetings with Jim?"

"No. Paul doesn't have to come and tell me

about all the times he speaks with every office woman at T&TEC. And I'm sure he sees women there, and he sees his apprentices' mothers who come to ask about their boys' progress. Paul is a handsome man, and I'm sure some of those apprentices' mothers are hitting on him."

"Do you read the comic strip—Mutt and Jeff?"

"Every day."

"You remember Mutt asked Jeff: 'If lightning strikes you once what is it? Jeff said it is an accident; Mutt asked, twice? Jeff said it's a coincidence; Mutt asked, thrice? Jeff said, It's a habit.'" Hilda looked at Ria and smiled. "You met Jim accidentally, coincidentally, or habitually?"

"I did not count."

The two idlers who heckled Ria the first day she went into Ross's sang aloud, "Big-mouth Hilda, ah go make a calypso on you."

"Frank and Harry, you are still peeing your bed? Come here and meet my friend, Ria"

When Ria and their eyes met, Frank shouted, "Oh, no!" Harry shouted louder, "Oh no!"

Ria got off the bench, and laughed nonstop.

Hilda said, "What is going on here with

you people?"

Ria, Frank, and Harry could not stop laughing.

Hilda shouted, "Could someone tell me what the hell is going on with you three fools?" She was terribly annoyed because she was left out of the joke.

Frank and Harry ran out of Woodford Square without saying a word to Hilda.

"Ria, you know my two cousins?" She was furious.

Ria controlled her laugher, but not completely. "I don't know them. The first day I came to work I met them at Ross's. They called me a country bookey coolie. They were wearing woollen shirts as if they just came from Alaska, and I told them to come to J.T.'s and I will buy them cotton shirts. A woman in the store ran out laughing with her coke and sandwich in hand. Other customers in Ross's were stifling their laughter."

"You made them look bad. I told them one day the joke will be on them. Let us come back to Jim. Do you have feelings for him?"

"What kind of feelings?"

"In this city that we call Port of Spain when we speak of having feelings for a man, we mean if you will go to bed with him."

"Just like that?"

"If he asks you to take a ride to Maracas Beach with him, would you go?"

"I'll never say never, but at this moment, the answer is no."

"All I will tell you is if any of those women at J.T.'s sees you with him at Maracas Beach, they will tell Magalange. Magalange's daughter is in love with him. J.T. Johnson doesn't have a trade union to protect its workers. That French Creole who has shares in J.T. will fire you as soon as you walk in and will have security walk you out. Your and Paul's dream of owning a house in St. James will die if Magalange knows of your interest in Jim. I rest my case. Thanks for giving me all of your commissions today."

"You are welcome."

"Ria, can I tell you a city woman's trick to use if you go to Maracas and park in the look-out? I don't know if Fyzabad's women know that trick."

"Only tell me if you have applied that trick

in the past and it worked for you."

"Whenever I like a guy, and I'm afraid if I go out with him, sit in the backseat of his car, and I may lose my control, and let him have his way, I put a tampon in before I leave home."

"Hilda, all Fyzabad's school boys and oil-field men know that trick. The men will pull out the tampon and make you smell it."

"Ria girl, don't say I didn't try to help if you lose control in the cold valley Maracas with Jim."

"You did try to help me, my friend. Check your diary for another trick and tell me the first thing tomorrow. Somehow, I think I'll be going with Jim for a ride to Maracas. Before my sister got married she told me she flirted with a boy, and it is a nice feeling. The next time I meet my sister I want to tell her that she has no more experience with a man than I."

"Your sister was lucky that, that Fyzabad man did not beat her up if she refused to give him sex. In this town, the men beat you up if you turn them on and then say no to sex. Good luck, Ria."

They got out of Woodford Square, and their laughter was echoed in the Anglican Cathedral on the western end of The University of Woodford Square.

On her way home, Ria was wondering whether she should tell Paul about Jim, and wondering more what she would tell Jim if he asked her out. Her mind was so full of lies. Those two men clogged her brain. She did not know to whom she should tell yes, and to whom she should tell no.

Everything in Port of Spain's society and culture was pushing her to be a friend of Jim's. Most nights she went in her bed before Paul and pretended she was sound asleep when he hugged her. Other nights she stood in front of the mirror, combed her long hair, put countless curlers in her hair, and waited till Paul fell asleep. She slept with her breasts on Paul's back and thought of herself and Jim driving to Maracas Beach.

One morning Aunt Nellie knocked.

"Come in, Aunt Nellie."

"Ria, I have a secret for you. Uncle Bassam is going to buy a Singer foot machine because he sees that the hand machine is giving you problem."

"Aunt Nellie, tell him he doesn't have to."

"The salesman will be bringing in the machine on Saturday. When you come home you can try it out, and sew a new dress from the cloth you bought at Sabga. My friends saw the dress you made for me, and they asked if they can give you jobs. Is that okay with you?"

"I'll let you know, Aunt Nellie."

The new gift didn't excite her. On her way home yesterday, she walked up Charlotte Street and read an advertisement in front of Sabga's Store: AMERICAN TWIGGY STYLES JUST ARRIVED. She stepped in the store and saw the dresses on mannequins. She had lost the five pounds that she hated on her body, and the mannequins were her size. The Twiggy dresses were what were in her mind when Aunt Nellie spoke of the new Singer machine. Something else was on her mind: The thought of her and Jim driving to and from Maracas Beach in the moonlight when Paul was working overtime to get money to buy their dream house in St. James.

Every Saturday she and Paul visited a new site, and she wrote it in her diary: She visited Caroni Swamp twice; Dattatreya Temple and Hanuman Statue; Emperor Valley Zoo; Mount

St. Benedict Monastery; National Museum and Art Gallery. Their biggest excitement was the steelband competition at Queens Hall when Dixie Land won the title. On their way home, they held hands; Paul whistled *The White Cliffs of Dover*; and she sang the words.

At bedtime Paul played his banjo; she was not in the mood for love; but she fitted herself on the bed with Jim on her mind.

"Ria," Paul began.

"Honey, you never call me Ria when we are in bed."

"My love, tomorrow I'm taking all of my apprentices for a treat after a football match in the park. After football, we are going to feast at Hot Shop Roti Shop, and some of the parents would be there. Would you like to come?"

"I'll *lime* (hang out) with Hilda till late."

"The apprentice who called me a country bookey, and his cute mother, a half breed, will be in the park. Aren't you afraid I'll fall in love with that beautiful half breed with long hair and long legs like yours?"

"Have a nice time, Paul."

"You too, my love. Give Hilda my regards."

In the morning Aunt Nellie knocked. Ria answered. "Come in."

"Where is my nephew?"

"He went in the savannah with his apprentices to play football."

"Come and see the new Singer machine; and there's someone I want to introduce you to."

"I can only stay for five minutes, because I'm on my way out."

She went upstairs, and Aunt Nellie introduced her to a friend. "Ria, meet an old friend of mine. Both of us taught at the same school for many years."

"My name is Ria Patel?"

"I am Telly Mason. So nice to meet you, Ria. Nellie speaks about you in glowing terms. She said you are an ace seamstress."

"Sometimes I butcher my frocks; sometimes I do a good job."

"I'm a seamstress too, but I do not have the time. I go to Fyzo very often to see my mother, Lyris George."

"I'm from Fyzo too. I'm very busy today because I have to meet a friend."

"Can you butcher a frock for me sometimes?"

"I surely will, when I have the time."

"I can take you wherever you want me to drop you to meet your friend."

"That is so kind of you, Lady Fyzo."

"My brothers, Tony and Lloyd…"

Ria cut her off. "Wait for me in your car. I will be out in a minute."

Ria was dressed in khaki shorts, light pink top tied at her waist, sandals, and a beach bag. But she covered the things in her bag with two magazines.

"Ria, tell me where to drop you."

"Drop me at the head of Frederick Street."

"We are coming close to it. Tell me when."

"Right here is fine. Thank you. I hope we meet again Telly to talk about Fyzo gossips." She walked to Marli Street, a car door opened, and she stepped in.

"I didn't believe you'd come."

"Jim, I'm here."

"Thanks for coming. I'm taking you on a trip with scenery that you'd never see in Fyzabad."

"I didn't come to hear you put down the

place where I was born."

"I like doing that to hear your cutting answers, Ria. Do you have a nickname?"

"Paul calls me coolie gal."

"And you don't get annoyed?"

"No."

"What do you call him?"

"Don't you think your questions are too personal?"

"I'm sorry. I heard a rumor about you is circulating at J.T.'s."

"What's it's all about?"

"Stop pretending, Ria. For the past year you won that award three times. I also heard you are a movie ambassador. And a certain man boasts about you at Country Club; and he told Magalange to put you in bookkeeping. Next month you will be upstairs in bookkeeping."

"How do you know that?"

"I have my spies. My spies say you are sartorially ready for any occasion. Why are you dressed like this today?"

"I dressed in these khaki shorts in case I have to run from you. By the way, why is it you are always at Ross's when I'm in there? Are you tracking me down?"

"Could be."

"I have spies too. My spies told me that you are in love with Maggie's daughter; and if Maggie knows you took me to Maracas Beach, she will fire me. Whose spies are better informed—yours or mine?"

He changed the conversation. "Do you like all the scenery so far?

"It's effable for words."

"Just like you."

They were on the North Coast Road, about forty minutes from Port of Spain on their way to Maracas Beach. The scenic drive through the mountainous rainforest exhibiting breathtaking views of the lush peninsulas jutting into the sea had Ria thinking of Paul writing a poem of the scenery dedicated to her. "The view is a nirvana of nature for lovers," she said softly, and rubbed her leg on Jim and pulled it away.

The deep precipices seen below had Jim's right foot tenderly on the brake. But Ria was somewhat afraid and she brought herself closer to Jim to be comforted from her fear. Jim was smiling because he had traveled on this road countless times; but Ria was afraid and felt that on most parts of the North Coast Road Jim's car could hardly pull away from the approaching heavy vehicles, and danger could be imminent. She was pressing her insteps so hard on the mat on the floor that the straps on her sandals burst when Jim negotiated a sharp corner overlooking another precipice. She felt hope of reaching Maracas Beach safely when she spotted Blazney Hill in the distance. The cold breeze descending from the giant trees on the hills blew into her bosom, and she liked the way the coldness of the breeze hardened her nipples. She wished Paul were next to her and fondling them. The shadows from the trees darkened the car, and she closed her eyes. When she opened them, Jim had already parked the Ford, and he was in his calypso bathing trunks.

He jumped into the water. "Ria, the water is warm and nice. Get in before the crowd from San Juan flocks in."

"The San Juan people and the Negroid Extracts are in war?"

He did not answer her question. Somehow, he felt Ria researched all facets of his life.

She changed into a slimming draped one-piece bathing suit that accentuated her figure. She jumped in and stayed under water. He looked for her. When she touched him, he said, "I got scared. I thought a shark swallowed you. You are not only good in salesmanship to cheat the other girls' award, you are also a fish without gills."

"Let's race for my award."

"What's your award?"

"A kiss on my cheek."

"To where?"

"To the shore. Take two yards advantage."

When she was having a snack, he was walking towards her, panting. "Where did you learn to swim that fast?"

"In Oropouche Sea."

"Where's that?"

"Down Fyzabad way. You lost, but I will still grant you a kiss on both cheeks."

He kissed her cheeks. "I have a case of cold beer in the trunk. I'm having one. Bring one for you?"

"I'm good."

"You don't drink beer?"

"No sort of alcohol."

"You are a teetotaler?"

"An ordained teetotaler."

"I've never heard that term. Is it Fyzabad's?"

"It's Ria's. I grew up with my Father who is a reformed drunkard. And I promised myself and him that I will never mess with any type of alcohol."

"Is your Father alive?"

"He is alive in Fyzo."

"I like the name. Paul is from Fyzo too?"

"Yes."

"He knows where you are?"

"No."

"Would he question you if he finds a wet bathing suit in your bag?"

"He would never search my bag. And if he sees a wet bathing suit hanging on the line to dry, he would not question me. Would Maggie's daughter do the same if she drops by you tonight and sees a wet trunk in your dirty-clothes basket?"

"I'm going in the car trunk to get another beer." He did not answer the question.

"Jim, let's take a walk along the beach and

play in the sand."

"You can go. I'm tired from that race you put me through."

"Thanks for staying where you are, and for not letting me lose my job should we be seen together by one of J.T.'s French Creoles." She looked back at him and smiled.

They went back into the water, and they swam horizontally along the beach to and from the spot where their clothes were. They dressed. Then he drove her to the lookout. No cars were parked with lovers that late evening.

"It is twilight, and the view all around us is heavenly. Come out the car with me. Maggie's spies are not here. I'll make it more comfortable for you. I'm going in the back seat and hide from my workmates."

He laughed.

"Jimmy boy, see how I'm making it easy for you not to lose your dowry from Mr. and Mrs. Magalange and for me not to lose my job. If I count to three, and you are not in the back seat, you'll get no loving from me. One, two."

"Am in."

He came close to her. "Can obedient me

kiss Fyzo's treasure?" He didn't wait for an answer. He kissed her deep. And she responded. Their romance was passionate for half an hour. "That's enough, Jimmy boy. Time to drive me home."

He slapped her twice, and hard. "I will obey you tonight. But not the next time."

She felt the blows but she did not cry. She shouted, "Reserve the next time for Maggie's daughter. What's that female Negroid Extract's name?"

He looked at her with scorn for knowing so much about his kith and kin. "Coleen is her name, bitch. What else you want to know?"

"Help me sing: *Little Man You've Had a Busy Day* slapping me."

"You love to mock men. I slapped your face, but the next man you torture will beat your coolie ass till you bleed."

"Jimmyboy, does that mean the nice Negroid Extract won't be having tea at Ross's with me any more?"

He stopped the car abruptly and drove off recklessly without saying a word to her except, "Get out! You stink coolie!"

She cussed him with her middle finger. She pushed the finger high, and deep.

Uncle Bassam was in the porch. "Ria, isn't that the famous golfer, Jim McBride?"

"That's he, Uncle Bassam."

"Where did you know him?"

"He is one of my best customers at J.T. Johnson. I was walking, he saw me, and he gave me a ride home."

She rushed into her apartment because she was afraid Uncle Bassam may ask her another question about Jim McBride if he sees the redness from Jim's hard slap on her sore face.

Paul was still out with an apprentice's mother enjoying an after football evening with wine, romance, and sex.

# 16

She couldn't wait for Monday to come to tell Hilda what took place on Maracas Beach. But Hilda had news for her too.

"Ria, I'm weeping inside."

"Who's dead in your family, Hilda—Frank or Harry?"

"You'll know soon."

A messenger approached her. "Are you Ria?"

"Yes, I am."

"Mrs. Magalange sent for you."

Ria told herself: *This is it. I had a nice time Sunday at Maracas Beach with Jim. Today I will be fired because of Jim.*

She knocked softly.

"Come in, Ria. Take a seat."

She sat.

"You had a nice weekend?"

"Good enough."

"What you did?"

"Nothing special."

"Where did you go?"

"Since I came from Fyzabad I took this weekend to do some sightseeing."

"Where did you go?"

"To Maracas." Her heart was pounding, not knowing what will follow.

"You went from Port of Spain or through San Juan along the Santa Cruz road through Petite Curucaye?"

"I don't know the geography of the surrounding, so I don't know where I was."

"Did you see the old Stollmeyer Estate?"

"The coldness around there was so intense that it put me to sleep." *Lord, I hope she believes me.*

"You missed a treat by not seeing the landscape."

"I assure you, Mrs. Magalange, the next

time I'll stay awake."

"I went to Henny's birthday party."

"Did you enjoy it?"

"Didn't you hear your name ringing in your ears?"

"Why should bells be ringing in my ears?"

"Henny was talking about you. Jack was talking about you. And sometime this week Jack will be bringing Henny to see you. By the way, how many movie houses are in Fyzabad?"

"Two—Ideal and Empire."

"When did you have time to go to so many movies? Didn't you have other hobbies?"

"My Father was a recovering alcoholic so the only thing to keep him away from the rum shops was to go to the movies, and he took my twin sister, Rena, and me when he went. And he went often. Rena and I were eight then, and we used to go home and write in a copy book all the movies we had seen. She had five copy books full, and I had seven."

"And today you showed off on me."

"Of course not, Mrs. Magalange. I simply answered the gentleman's question. He treated me as a human being, not as a nobody, as other customers have treated Hilda and me: They think we are not of their ilk and breeding."

Margaret Magalange was silent for more than a minute. When she spoke, she sounded as Mother Theresa showering her blessings to the natives she befriended in India. "Ria, I want you and Coleen to know each other, not as employees, but as friends. Do you know she's my daughter?"

"I was told so."

"Ria, I called Oxford Commercial College, and your principal, Mr. Donaldson, and I spoke at length. He told me when he was the Alderman and the Mayor of San Fernando, you sat in as principal for him. And you did a good job teaching the students in his absence. You never wrote those things in your application. Why?"

"I thought you'd think I'm over qualified for this job."

Mrs. Magalange looked at her and gave a half smile. "I promised you three years ago when a vacancy comes up you'd be the first one to fill it. Didn't I say that?"

"Yes, Mrs. Magalange."

"Did you believe me?"

"With a grain of salt."

"And some masala?"

Ria smiled.

"On Monday, walk straight upstairs, and Coleen will tell you what is to be done as a bookkeeper. That's it."

"Thank you. I'm grateful for your trust in me."

The day was over

She and Hilda went to Ross's. They looked at each other before they ordered.

"I'm treating you, Hilda."

"I expect the bookkeeper on the upper floor to go into her purse. But I want Chinese."

The attendant came. "Can I help you, ladies?"

"No. My big sister wants Chinese; and I don't want a certain man to meet me here so I have to leave."

As they sit down at the Chinese restaurant at the corner of Frederick and Park Street, Ria spoke. "Girl, I had my test with Jim McBride."

"When?"

"Sunday."

"Where?"

"On the North Coast Road, and in the beach."

"Both of you were in the water?"

"Yes."

"With clothes on?"

"I had on a black one-piece bathing suit."

"What he had on?"

The waiter came. "What you want to drink with your meal?"

"Two cokes," Ria answered. "And we'll order later...Girl, he had on a multi-colored bathing trunk."

"What else you did?"

"We had swimming races; and I beat him in all the races."

"Is he as handsome in his bathing trunk?"

"He has a beautiful body."

The waiter came back. "You ready to eat?"

Hilda answered. "You want us to leave and go somewhere else. I will tell you when we are ready to eat." And she continued. "Did you touch his body in the water?"

"In the water, and on land."

"Where on land?"

"By the lookout."

"In the back seat?"

"In the back seat."

"He's a good kisser?"

"Very good kisser."

"He got your forbidden fruit?"

"Only Paul gets that."

"Would you tell Paul?"

"Maybe."

"So on Sunday you had kisses; and now you are leaving me. I don't think I want Chinese food. I'm sad that you'll be leaving me."

"I'll order take out for both of us."

"Ria, I told Frank and Harry to keep an eye on you and protect you. I told them to tell all the boys in the steelband."

"Who are these boys in the steelband?"

"You don't have to know them. They will know you."

Each had her takeout in hand; Ria stopped a taxi, and the cabbie dropped off Hilda first.

The door was opened ajar, and there was Paul with his red rose in hand. She put down his dinner and kissed him.

"Paul, I cannot wait till tonight."

"Me too."

They behaved as if it was the first time they made love. Their sex rugged. Their sex was not gentle. Their behavior made them tiresome. Their behavior had them locked in each other's arms. Then she spoke.

"My love, on Monday I'll be kicked upstairs to bookkeeping."

"My only love, soon we'll be living in St. James, and I will be romancing you with a roti every day instead with roses."

"Once I hear your footsteps every day, with or without rose and roti, that's all I need."

"All I need is to eat my Chinese."

They ate their Chinese takeout without clothes on.

Two weeks later, she got up one morning and touched him. "Paul, I had expected my period last month, and I did not see it yet."

He shouted, "Hurrah for Oliver!"

"Who is Oliver?"

"My first born that the stalk put inside your belly. Next week we will be married in the doors of court. I want to say, 'My wife,' instead of that 'Coolie gal from Fyzabad.'"

"Would you tell Aunt Nellie and Uncle

Bassam that I'm one month pregnant?"

"As soon as I get dressed."

"I'll be going upstairs to sew a dress for Aunt Nellie, and then I will tell both of them."

"And I will write Alex, and warn him not to tell Mother."

"And I will write Rena and tell her to tell Ziffo but not to tell Madame Joe. Rena wrote me last week, and she told me that she's pregnant. I didn't tell you because she had so many miscarriages. She's having a girl in January."

"My first born will have to come out of you in my bedroom in Fyzabad."

"I want Nurse Awon to deliver me, and I want you in the delivery room."

"Not me. If I see the forbidden fruit, I would not want to eat it again."

"Honey, do you want to be my psychiatrist for a day?"

"Yeah! And do you want to be my psychiatrist for a day, too?"

"Yeah! You be my psych first."

"Okay. I will sit on the bed, and you must put your head in my lap."

She did it.

"Ria, you or your psychiatrist must show no emotions no matter what his or her client says. Is that understood?"

"That's understood. That is very fair, Dr. Sears. You will not reproach me, neither will I."

"Coolie gal, you ever loved a nigger man?"

"Just one."

"What's his name?"

"Doctor, I will tell you in my next visit."

"Coolie gal, do white men or Negroid Extracts stop you on the street and say you are beautiful?"

"Yes."

"What's his name?"

"I will tell you that in my next visit, Dr. Sears."

"Did you date him?"

"Yes."

"Where did you go?"

"Maracas Beach."

"Did you go in the water with him?"

"Yes."

"Were you close in the water with him?"

"Yes."

"What else you did?"

"He parked by the lookout, Dr. Sears."

"In the back seat?"

"Yes."

"What you did?"

"Pulled out his tonsils."

"He pulled out your tonsils, too?"

"Yes. But it was very painful, Dr. Sears."

"What else was painful?"

"He slapped me very hard because I would not let him pull off my panty?"

"Did he get it off?"

"No. Now you'd be my patient."

"Okay." He lay in her lap.

"Fyzabad nigger, who was your girlfriend before Ruby?"

"A Chinese girl."

"Where was her Father's shop?"

"At the beginning of Delhi Road."

"One of Mongs's daughters?"

"Yes, Dr. Patel."

"Mong has three daughters—Kim, Aming, and Amoy—which one?"

"I will tell you in my next visit, Dr. Patel."

"Since you have left Fyzabad and you are now living in this city, you ever had a woman?"

"Yes."

"You had sex with her?"

"Yes, Dr. Patel."

"Who is she?"

"One of the apprentices' mothers."

"What's her address?"

"Dr. Patel, I will tell you that in my next visit."

"Get off of me! Now! Now! Now!" She shouted and he got up and sat on the floor. "You could have prevented things from happening to your body by using your mind and thinking of me. All you Fyzabad men—young, middle aged, and old—are the same no good. Don't come on my bed tonight or any other night. I wish I had Zoffi Thakur's blade to put your blood on it."

She did not speak to him in two weeks.

At work Coleen said, "Ria, all we do is sit here and work for this ungrateful company. We never spend time and discuss our family life. I like you, Ria, and I don't care whether or not you like me. Today I'm in the mood to talk about me. Guess who gave me this coconut-sized diamond?"

"It's really big like a dry coconut. Who?"

"Jim McBride. He is an actuary."

"What he does?"

"A sort of consultant work. He stays home and works for many insurance companies, and he tells insurance companies what plans to give their buyers. He makes a lot of money. He's a consultant for J.T.J. Do you know him?"

"I've seen his photo in the sports page many times."

"Would you come to my wedding?"

"When?"

"In November."

"In November, I will be delivering my first born in Fyzabad."

"What! You got married to Paul?"

"Last week, in the doors of court."

"Would you like J.T. Johnson to give you a baby shower before you leave?"

"I prefer an extended maternity leave."

"I'll tell Mom. She'd be happy to do that."

"You and I got hit below the navel in March. You got pregnant, but I didn't."

"Seems that way, girl. Coleen, I was entering some sales in the journal, and I noticed there was not a double entry for some items. Is there a reason for that?"

"That will be taken care of."

"Okay. You are in charge."

On her way home, Ria was thinking of Paul's confession, and she wondered if she were stupid not to let Jim go all the way. She quickened her steps. She wanted to be home as soon as Paul stepped in the house. She was home before him, and she cooked because whenever he comes home first, he cooks a sumptuous dinner. As soon as Paul stepped in the door and handed her a red rose, she shouted, "Take it to your whore. Her son called you a country bookey. The country bookey had to show the city whore the size of his balls. After the football match, you slept with her. I should have allowed Jim to do it with me."

"We agreed with each other that our confession would end and not be spoken of in reproach."

"You promised to be faithful to me till death."

"Dr. Patel, my psychiatrist, you are unfair."

"I am not. Don't you think I was enjoying Jim's caresses? But I did not let my body rule my head. You must have let your body rule your head every night that you told me that you were working late to get money to buy a house in St. James. You got your overtime money from her hairy bank somewhere in this dirty Port of Spain."

"Ria, don't bite the hand that feeds you. All Fyzabad did for you was birth you."

Her love for Paul was so strong that she spent the night in his arms after she quarreled with him; and she apologized for saying she will use Thakur machete on his neck. Their sex was not in the Christian pose that night. It was good.

Their topic after their romance was about their baby that is expected in November, and they should be ready when Reynold James comes to take them to Fyzabad in the morning.

Of the Fyzabad Terrible Trio, Reynold James was the most punctual; Anthony George was the most humorous and political; and Steve Crooks was equally political as Anthony, but he was the best cook. Paul wished the Trio were together on the trip to "home sweet home" to remind them how they ran from Boolitan's coolie gun; and to commend Steve of his genius with coining the COOLIE-GUN slogan which became a part of Fyzabad's lexicon.

Reynold and Paul could not stop talking about days gone by: about Bag-O-Sugar. Reynold said, "I used to tease Bag-o-Sugar every day. And she used to tell me, 'You is a horn child. Your mother don't know who your father is.'"

Paul spoke. "Raymond, she told me the same thing, and I went home and asked my Mother, 'Mother, what is a horn child? Alex and I are *horned children*?'"

"Paul you asked your Mother in the Queen's English: *horned children*." Reynold stopped the car because he could not control his laughter. Then he started the car. The car rocked with laughter on the one-mile creek road five miles from Fyzabad.

Ria joined in with more trash talk. "I teased her one morning when I was going to school in uniform, and what she told me I will never forget it, because I memorized it to tell girls who teased me in Telemaque's school: 'You, coolie girl in uniform, why to think your mother died so early? Your mother took nigger wood for money so she could buy school uniforms for you and your sister. Your hair is not even straight as coolie people."

"Ria, that's why your hair is curly like nigger hair. That is the result of nigger wood." Reynold said.

More laughter.

Paul wanted to hit back Reynold for teasing his wife. "Tobago nigger, I'm so sorry Boolitan didn't shoot you with his coolie gun."

"Paul, you did the right thing to take up for your first and last wife," Ria slammed Reynold with more trash talk. "Could you imagine that Tobago nigger who used to buy undersized *washikong* (sneakers) in Bata to save a penny is talking about my hair? Reynold, you used to cut the front of your *washikong* because it used to burn you and your jiggers like hell. Then you threw away the *washikong* and told your Mother the dog ate them."

Paul wanted to further help his wife's chastisement of Reynold. "Reynold, I never knew your feet were stinker than Tony and Steve's put together."

Their laughter brought them to Avocat village where there is a preponderance of East Indians. Reynold said, "I remember coming here as a boy to see an Indian man hanging from a rope. The rumor was a Creole man was boning his wife."

Paul shouted, "Reynold, stop here. I'm going to buy a newspaper." The headline on the *Trinidad Guardian* was bold: JAMES MC-BRIDE, GENIUS GOLFER, DIED IN A CAR CRASH ON THE WINDING NORTH COAST ROAD. He folded the paper and put it in his bosom. Then he bought two pealed oranges and a magazine. He held one orange and the magazine with his left hand close to his chest, and he handed Ria the other orange with his right hand. "Honey, these oranges are sweet. I'm sure the baby is craving for them."

"Paul, where is the newspaper?"

"That is stale news?"

"I saw when you bought a newspaper."

"I put it back and bought this magazine."

"I did not see when you put the newspaper back."

"Honey, I did."

"Then why was that boy selling outdated news?"

"In Avocat, people buy stale newspapers to wrap up stuff."

"That's true. My father is a butcher, and he uses old newspapers to wrap up meat for his customers."

Paul was shocked by the news. He had no appetite to make jokes and trash talk. He told Reynold that he is going to sleep in his wife's arms and to wake them up when they reach Gower's Well Road. "Reynold, ask me two more questions before I fall asleep."

"Who is called the Korean in Fyzabad?"

"Everybody knows who."

"Do you still play your banjo?"

Ria answered for her husband. "He can only play *The White Cliffs of Dover* on it."

"Ria, whenever I go by Paul's Mother to pick caimete (star apple), she's always singing that song when she's washing. Sometimes neighbor Thakur is there keeping her company and throwing water in the tub."

"You know he is my sister's husband?"

"I wonder if he still wants to put Paul's blood on his coolie blade."

"Reynold, his wife is making a baby. I'm

sure the joy of his new born burned completely his hatred for Paul. Wake me up when I reach twenty footsteps from my Mother-in-law's gate."

They were at the mound of the little incline by neighbor Elaine's house and Paul was struck by what he saw. "Ria, neighbor Elaine and neighbor Lyris are not cursing over land boundary, and the land is not theirs."

"Is that true?"

"They curse in their sleep too. Today is Thursday, and my Mother is not below the house washing my Father's clothes."

"Paul, we may have to sit on the bench below the house. And in case my water burst, what can I do? It is the first time I'm coming here. You don't have a phone. You don't have a key to your parents' house to get in."

"My Mother is living in this house for over forty years. Neighbor Lyris is the first house built in this area when only Roseau (a prickly tree) was here. Neighbor Lyris and my Mother never closed their doors."

"They are not afraid of thieves?"

"They are poor people. They have nothing in their houses to lose, but their poverty; and nobody will steal their poverty because theirs will be less than the thief's. So push the door hard, my dear."

She pushed it.

"Welcome home, Mr. Paul Sears and Mrs. Ria Patel-Sears!"

They were the people of Gower's Well Road, the graveled road, and Delhi Road who shouted in joy for Paul and Ria's expected appearance.

Madam Joe hugged her son. "My first born, I missed you." She pulled Ria into her hugging. "Ria, I love you. I heard so much about you from my sister, Nellie. In every letter she said, 'God made you for Paul.' And every night I prayed for you and Paul. I bought a new Singer foot machine, and I've bought clothes for you to sew for me before you go back to work at J.T Johnson in Port of Spain."

Ria answered. "Mother, I love you too. I will do my best for you to love me as much as your first born loves me."

Ria's Father hugged his daughter, and touched her belly softly. "My little Chookoo, I prayed for this day to come." He kissed her many times on both cheeks.

Paul let go his Mother, hugged his Father, and said, "Father, forgive me for not writing all these years. I love you, and I did not know what to put in my letter."

"You are a man, Paul. You don't have to make excuses."

Alex pulled Paul from their Father. "Soon you'll be having a young'un. When you knocked Ria up?"

"I heard your Mother and Father attended your wedding, and you knocked up Kristen, too."

Rena and Ria never ended their hugging. "So the twins are pregnant." Both said the identical words, and laughed aloud.

All the neighbors' gifts for the expected baby were in plastic bags on the table.

"I have an announcement to make, Paul."

"What is it neighbor Zoffi? Please, don't surprise me and make me cry."

"Your Father was not feeling well, so I painted the baby's room blue."

"Neighbor Zoffi, how do you know my room should be painted blue, and not pink?"

"My loving wife, Rena, told me all the secret news that came from Port of Spain. Come hold my hand, Paul." Paul held his hand. "Close your eyes, Paul, and follow me." He led Paul to his wife. "Touch this." Paul touched it. "That's my new born expected here in January. She's a girl."

Paul hugged Zoffi, and said, "We knocked up those sisters. Now we are even. Let's drink to that before Nurse Awon comes."

Nurse Awon was there in half an hour and addressed the crowd.

"Fyzo people, I'm Nurse Awon. I'm here to do an urgent examination on Mrs. Sears. Please, leave now. You can come back and show the baby's gifts to the new Sears family. I was Alex and Paul's midwife." She did her examination. "Mrs. Sears…."

"Please, call me Ria."

"Ria, your baby dropped very low. You may have it tonight or tomorrow. No walking about. No quarreling with your Mother-in-Law. No quarreling with your husband. I delivered him, and he peed on me when he was born." Nurse Awon put her stethoscope on Ria's navel. "Tomorrow this time your baby will be here."

She left and walked down the muddy incline by Elaine Trotman and spoke to herself. "I don't want to fall. I have another delivery when I leave here."

Paul went into the bedroom and kissed his wife's belly. "Tomorrow between this time and midnight, you will be pushing out Oliver Jimmyboy Sears, my first born."

"Why are you teasing your wife, Paul?"

"On our son's birth certificate will have the names Oliver James Sears."

"I will call him Jim."

"My loving wife, that will be your preference. Nurse Awon said no quarreling. Go to sleep."

# 17

It was the tenth day of November, a cool morning. The dew drops were still on the water grass like little bubbles in motion and Paul, remembering his childhood, jumped barefooted on the grass, and he knew what the temperature of the day would be. As a boy, he jumped on the dewy grass to know if rain would fall or if he would have to go and bring water from Johnny's well. He had liked to go to get water from Gower's well quarter mile away more than at Johnny's well which was closer. At Gower's well Ruby got her water there, and she brought sugar cakes for him.

He walked slowly to the spot where he

could see the pumping jack and to remind himself that he once rode on that pumping jack that Kenneth Dixon lost his leg on. The angled sun cast its rays on the slanted glasses on his nose bridge and neighbor Lyris called out. "Paul, I'm digging some sticky dasheen for Madam Joe to cook for you and your new wife."

"Thank you, neighbor Lyris."

Elaine wanted to drown the sound of Lyris' voice. She drowned it. "Paul, don't listen to that Grenadian woman. She eats the alligators that come in her yard. Come and pick pommerac. They are very sweet. I have a long rod below the house."

Ulric Dublin called, and Paul answered, "Boong, what's up?" Ulric got the nickname Boong when he was walking over a dam on a wet pipeline to go for cocorite, and he fell in the dam. The sound of his body on the still water was "boong." Boong is on his ID. The village knows him only as Boong.

"Paul, I heard you married that coolie woman who lived in Dehli Road."

"Boong, my wife's name is Mrs. Ria Patel-Sears. She is a bookkeeper at J.T. Johnson.

Country bookey, I'm sure you don't know where J.T. Johnson is?"

"I will tell your coolie wife about how you let out the wind from Teacher Randolph's bike tire because he took away your girlfriend, Ruby. You stopped eating for six months because you had a bad dose of *tabanka* (a lover's sadness for being jilted)."

When the boys and girls of Fyzabad who grew up in Gower's Well Road and its immediate surroundings meet, their teasing one another and trash talk is nonstop. Calling each other nigger or coolie is done with love and endearment.

Paul returned to his house with two dasheens and a paper bag full of pommeracs.

Thakur called out. "Paul, sit below the house on the bench that I always sit on. I'm bringing a bottle of Vat, the best rum from Fernandez brewery."

"Walk with two glasses because Nurse Awon doesn't want me upstairs. She only wants Rena and Madam Joe upstairs."

As Thakur sat on his favorite spot on the bench, Paul handed him a cigar and said, "Only light this cigar when you hear my son's voice."

"I hope you will never let your son become an acolyte like you of that athetist, John Jules." Thakur lights his cigar.

"Man, you couldn't wait for my first born to see the world before you light your cigar?"

"This is Cuban cigar. I couldn't wait."

It was one minute to midnight. Paul and Thakur heard a sound as a mother slapping her misbehaved child. It wasn't a misbehaved child who was slapped. The slap was from Nurse Awon; and the baby screamed on the stroke of midnight.

Paul screamed louder: "My first born is here. Neighbor Ziffo Thakur, run through your garden. Run through the short cut. Go and make noise with your machete on the grinding stone to announce the birth of Oliver James Sears to all the people of Gower's Well Road, the graveled road, and Delhi Road."

Thakur rushed through his garden, the shortest route to his house. He opened every door and every window and put his machete blade full speed on the grinding stone. The sound of his machete on the hot stone came down to the baby's room loud and clear. Thakur shouted over and over to the villagers who walked by, "Madam Joe has a grandson! His name is Oliver James Sears. I am his uncle. People, you hear me? I am his uncle. He is my nephew!"

"Paul, stop shaking as a mad man. Put on this coat. Now go and wash your face and hands thoroughly," Nurse Awon said.

"I'm finished, Nurse Awon."

"Did you wash your hands from your elbows down?"

"Yes, Nurse Awon."

"Here's your first born. Hold him carefully. He is only seven pounds."

Paul held his son high in the air as burnt offering. "Thank you, God, for giving my beautiful wife a safe delivery with little pain, and for letting my first born, Oliver James Sears, to be born in my parents' house. This house was once made of mud, grass, and strips, and now it is a beautiful board house. Thank you, God, for giving my parents long life. And, dear Lord, did you know my Mother and Father came from Tobago, and they are married for fifty three years?"

Madam Joe held her grandson, cradled him in her arms, and sang: *There'll be bluebirds over/ The White Cliffs of Dover/ Tomorrow/ Just you wait and see.*

Paul picked up his banjo and accompanied his Mother as she sang and smiled.

One month later, Paul rested the newspaper he had hidden from Ria on the dinner table, but he stood nearby. She read the headline, and screamed endlessly.

Paul held her tenderly. "My love, he had no pain. He died instantly. He has gone to meet his Maker in heaven."

"Jim was a lovely man, Paul."

"To be your friend, he had to be more than a lovely man, Ria. Close the bedroom door and cry as loud as you wish. My parents will never ask you why are you crying."

"Paul, I'm not going back to Port of Spain. We'll build our house here in Omaree's Park."

"Whatever you say, my little Chookoo."

"Now you and my Father will be calling me by my nickname. Stay with me until I fall asleep, Paul."

"Whatever you say, my loving…."

"Don't say that word!"

They laughed and looked at their handsome baby in his crib.

"Mother and Dad, Paul and I will not be going back to live in Port of Spain."

"Ria, did both of you tell Alex?"

"Mother, Alex already knows. He wants us to build a house next to him and Kirsten in Omaree's Park."

"Welcome home, Mr. and Mrs. Sears," Madam Joe and Joseph said. Joseph walked away grinning.

Ria hugged and kissed Madam Joe. "I thank you, Mother. I will no longer miss my other Mother who died when I was five years old."

Ria wiped Madam Joe's tears.

"Ria, it makes me cry with joy when opposites come together and discard their hatred of each other. I never thought this day would come." Madam Joe spoke softly. "Ria, did you read the uncharitable letters I wrote to Paul? If you did, please, forgive me for what I said."

"I did not read any."

Paul took his wife into their bedroom, and he wiped her tears.

"I love you, Ria. Do you love me as much as I love you?"

"Shut up, Paul. Jim is crying. Hurry! Bring him to me, and then put your shoes where they belong."

"Lord, another Jim in my life to make me jealous. I hate the name Jim."

"What did you say, Paul?"

"I was talking to myself about Jim's future civic engagements."

"You are lying, Paul!" She looked at him." I will no longer call my son Jim. I will call him Paul Jr."

"Thank you, my love."

## About the Author

**Lloyd Hollis Crooks** was born in the Republic of Trinidad and Tobago, West Indies.

He is the author of *Blood on the Blade; Peeping Through The Keyhole; Ice and Eyes in the Sun - True Love Comes Late, Sometimes;* and *Grenada Ghost.*

Crooks covered "sensitive" national and international conferences in the Office of the Prime Minister during the Dr. Eric Williams Administration. He also worked as a Court Reporter, and a Parliament (Hansard) Reporter. In New York, he was a Legal Assistant in two Wall Street law firms.

His Books and Kindle Edition can be obtained at Amazon.com ~ *See website: lloydholliscrooks.com*